PostPartum
By

GJ Coleman

www.gjcoleman.com

PostPartum

‑

ISBN-978-0-6151-7568-3
Library of Congress Control Number: 2007909022

PostPartum

ACKNOWLEDGEMENTS
This book is dedicated to my family, Ronald, Jonathan, L. Joy, April, Tiffani and Kara. Thanks for the journey. A special thanks to Doctor's Jesse & Halene Giddens for teaching me how to love God with all of my heart, my mind and my spirit. Thank you for being real.

PostPartum

**For there is nothing covered that shall
not be revealed; neither hid, that
shall not be known**   Luke 12:3 KJV

Prologue

"I'm going inside, and don't try to stop me."

"It's your career!" David was tired of trying to protect His Honor. All of his advice fell on deaf ears. The mayor had let this girl drag him into the gutter, and he could kiss his career goodbye if one of the snoopy reporters from the *Desert Den* got wind of what he was doing. If he wanted to give it all up for a piece of young tail, then so be it.

The windshield wipers were now just slopping water from one side of the windshield to the other, the rain coming down too hard for them to be of any effect. Water poured from the sky and rushed through the streets like an angry river, ripping signs from doors and pushing debris everywhere.

The mayor was being a fool, but he'd obviously already made the decision to go inside no matter what David said. David lit a cigarette and leaned back for the long wait. He knew that babies came when they were ready, that the due date was only an estimated time of arrival. His daughter had taken twenty-seven hours to make her grand entrance into the world. By the time the mayor's kid arrived, somebody could find out what His Honor was up to just by accidentally stepping in his path. David only knew that he didn't want *his* picture plastered across the front page of the *Den*. His wife was already giving him grief about being gone so much, and if she discovered he was complicit in the mayor's dirty activities, things would get much worse for him on the home front. Jeanette hated the great Andrew Blake.

They had all attended high school together, and for some reason unbeknownst to David, Jeanette, who was his girlfriend since their junior year, had taken an instant dislike to Andrew.

Andrew had been destined for greatness since high school, however. He was an honor-roll student and valedictorian of their graduating class. Although David's childhood friend was always in the middle of some kind of drama, fighting battles long before his tenure as mayor, if word leaked out that he was having an affair with his secretary's niece slash volunteer worker, his name would be mud in Juniper. David was afraid this particular drama may not play out the way the mayor had planned, but only time would tell. David just hoped he didn't get drug through the muck right along with him.

"You'll have to walk from here so the car isn't spotted. Do you know the room number?"

"Four-twenty-one. The old woman called me as soon as she went into labor. Her sister has the adjoining room and is ready to move."

"Would it do any good to tell you to just walk away?" David asked, pulling the car to a complete stop by the back entrance of the hotel.

"No!" It was obvious that no one could stop him from being present when his first child was born.

Andrew trudged through the rain to the hotel's back door. A man was waiting to escort him through the back hall to room four-twenty-one. The old woman had left the door open for them. The small dining area was dark except for what little light escaped under the bedroom door. Andrew stripped off his black slickers and galoshes and set them by the vent to dry. An older woman with a turban wrapped around her head slipped out of the bedroom door and pulled it shut.

The woman didn't look so old in person. He had been told she was sixty, but she didn't look a day over forty. Her skin was as smooth as silk, her teeth pearly white, and she moved around the room with the agility of a panther. He didn't know any sixty-year-olds who moved like that. He could barely move like that, and he worked out every day.

"She just startin' ta push now. Cain't rush naycha," the old woman said, looking around as if there was something missing. Andrew knew that he need not worry about her trying to identify him. The woman had been a midwife for more than thirty years and had made next to nothing for all the babies she had brought into the world. She just wanted to get her hands on the money he had promised her. A smile crept across her face when she thought of the sum he was willing to pay to have her perform her craft. The man who had escorted the mayor up to the room shifted from one foot to the other, waiting for the transaction to take place so he could be compensated for his role.

"Mah package, suh?" the old woman said with an outstretched hand. Andrew reached into his pocket, withdrew the envelope, and handed it to her. She counted the contents, passed the escort his portion, and scampered back inside the room like a child with a new toy. The escort found a place on the couch and watched as the mayor paced back and forth.

PostPartum

The moans from inside the bedroom were getting louder now. Andrew could hear a voice other than the old woman's consoling the girl. He assumed it was the girl's sister. He knew he was a fool for being here, just like David said he was, but he couldn't keep himself away. Besides, he had instructed the old woman on the phone to notify him when the baby was out of the womb and crying, but she had called sooner than he had expected.

CHAPTER 1

Andrew had waited forty-eight years for a child of his own. His wife of ten years, Angie, was barren, or so she said, and thus could not give him the one thing he wanted so badly. He had begged her to find a fertility doctor and try some of the new techniques, but Angie had quickly dismissed his request. "Nobody is going to make me alter my body so I can end up with one of those freaks that ride the short bus," she had blurted out to end one of their many arguments. He knew not to press any harder after that. Once Angie made up her mind about something, she got her way. That's how they had ended up together.

Angie was a truly a fine looking woman and she knew it. Her large brown eyes and curvy shape had kept Andrew and many others sniffing around her like bloodhounds on a trail. She refused his first two offers for a date, but true to form, she became very interested when he gave up and started dating one of the cheerleaders from a rival school. She had pursued him like he was the President of the United States after that.

Angie had shown him things in bed that he had never experienced before. He was too busy enjoying the benefits to question how she came by her abilities. His friends teased him and said his nose was "wide open," but he didn't care. As soon as they were married and he took a seat on the City Council, however, she snatched the rug from under him, letting him know just how little she cared for him. Her place in their small community secure, he was no longer needed. She had played him, and he had willingly conceded his freedom and his happiness to a shrew.

There were rumors that Angie was sneaking about with the physical therapist at the health club she attended, but when he confronted her, she had denied any infidelity and swore everyone was jealous of her. The sad truth was that Andrew could care less what she was doing as long as she stayed out of his way. She had become someone to be tolerated, and she was to blame for that sad state of affairs. Early in their marriage, he had tried many times to get her to spend more time with him at home and on the road, but she was always too busy with her own activities. He gave up a long time ago.

He couldn't believe that the girl he had fallen madly in love with was the same woman who now haunted his days. His mother had taken an instant dislike to Angie and had warned him about her, but Andrew

PostPartum

was too far gone by the time his mother tried to intervene. Now she was just a sorry mistake, an albatross, a royal pain in His Honor's backside.

CHAPTER 2

When Andrew came back to campaign headquarters late one night to go over his speech for an upcoming debate, Lila, his secretary's niece, was still in the office working at the computer.

"Hey, Mister Mayor," she had said, smiling as she pecked out something on the computer. He hadn't recognized her at first. She had on a long white halter dress and her hair had been pinned up in a cluster of curls. The halter had a V-shaped front that showed her cleavage, which he had not noticed existed until that moment. Her caramel skin glowed under the white dress.

"I'm not the mayor yet," he replied as he tried to break his gaze long enough to unlock the door to his small office. When he finally got the door open, he rushed in so he wouldn't make a complete idiot of himself.

"What had happened to the jeans and t-shirt she wore like a uniform each day?" he mumbled to himself.

"Are you talking to somebody, Mr. Blake?" Lila asked, appearing in front of him like a dream. He turned away from her before she could see his expression.

"I was talking to myself. You start to do that when you get old."

"Well I must be old 'cause I talk to myself all the time," she said, and then she laughed lightly, making his heart skip a beat. He told himself he must be really horny to think about this young girl in that way. Angie had been gone for a week, and before she left, she feigned some sort of sickness to avoid any sexual contact between them. A soft breeze would make his soldier stand to attention right about now.

"Why are you still here, Lila?" he snapped without meaning to.

"I forgot to finish something Auntie Barb told me to do. So I borrowed her key and came back to get it done. I'm almost finished, if that's what you're worried about.

"I'm sorry to snap at you. It's just been a long day, and I have that debate tomorrow, which is wearing on me." He sat down behind his desk. He needed a lot of space between him and the beautiful creature in the doorway. He was at least thirty years her senior. Barbara hadn't told him how old her niece was, but he assumed she was eighteen or nineteen because she had just graduated from high school. Lila walked into Andrew's office.

"I accept that apology, but don't let it happen again," she said with a tone of mock indignation. "I'm your most devoted employee." She was now perched on the edge of the desk, driving him crazy without realizing it.

"And how did you get that title," he asked as he made a Herculean attempt to relax. It was okay to acknowledge a pretty young girl, he told himself. He hadn't broken any laws.

"I come to work with my aunt three times a week, and I work all hours of the day and night and don't get a dime. That's how."

He laughed out loud then. "You've got a point there. How about I find a position for you in the big house if I get elected?" She was up and had her arms around his neck before he knew it. Her full breasts bounced inside the silky material as if they would burst out at any moment.

"I'm sorry about that," she said as she backed away, "but just the thought of working for the mayor is too cool." She rubbed the lipstick off his cheek with her finger. "I wouldn't want you to get in trouble with your wife for a simple kiss of gratitude."

"Thank you. I wouldn't have thought to wipe it away. It's not every day a pretty young girl kisses me.

"I wonder why. You must notice that all the females in the office make eyes at you when you come into the building. They all say you're fine for an old man."

"I know you're just trying to make me feel better, and I thank you, but I better let you head off to wherever you were going. I know you're not dressed like that to type boring campaign memos."

"Actually, I had some pictures taken today. I haven't had pictures made since grade school."

"Well, I'm sure they'll be beautiful. You're a very pretty girl."

"Girls go to elementary school. I'm a woman, in fact, I turned eighteen today."

"I beg your pardon, Miss Lila, and happy birthday. Shouldn't you be out partying with some of your friends?"

"It's hard to make friends in a small town like Juniper. I have a few acquaintances, but that's it. The last year in high school was a nightmare. The guys were friendly enough, but the females were *"trippin'."* I only had one true friend, and she went off to college already. The rest of my friends are guys. It's easier to hang out with them."

"Well, those females, as you call them, were just jealous. How 'bout, since you are my most devoted employee, I take you to a restaurant to celebrate your birthday. Call your aunt and see if she'll join us." Andrew figured he better add someone else to the mix before he did something he would regret.

"No!" Lila said quickly.

"Wha...," Andrew started to say before she cut him off.

"Let's order in and eat here. We don't need Auntie Barb. She's probably asleep anyway."

"Uh, well okay then — it's *your* birthday. What do you want to eat?"

"Let's have some soul food from Nate's. He's got the bomb chicken and rice."

"Nate's it is." Andrew lay down his speech and cleared his desk while Lila ordered the meal.

"It's ordered. Now, come on old man." Leave that work and let's go watch the DVD I brought. Lila pulled Andrew into the break room. "It's some stupid movie about a football team striking and some other guys filling in. It looked like a good comedy. You need to lighten up."

"Okay, birthday girl. It's your night." Andrew followed Lila into the small room that had been converted into a makeshift employee lounge with a couch, small table and chair, microwave, and television mounted on the wall so the workers could relax after a long day of work.

Andrew's father owned the small building, and he had offered it to him when he needed a place for his campaign headquarters. Lila stood on a chair and put the tape into the VCR. She jumped down, every sweet bounce and jiggle making Andrew cringe, and joined him on the couch.

"I'll get the door when the food comes. We don't want the public to think you're having an affair."

"No we don't. They'd kick my butt right out of here tomorrow." They both laughed.

"I've told you all about my sad high school days, but I don't know anything about you except that you are going to be mayor and have this fine wife who never comes down here unless the cameras are rolling that day." Lila had pretty much summed his life up and there was nothing else to tell. He had stopped having a life when he entered public office. Angie had her status and he had his victories. Case closed.

"There's nothing to tell, really," Andrew said, pretending to watch the previews.

"Do you have any kids?"

"No."

"Why not?" Andrew didn't want to get into the specifics of his life, and he wished she'd change the subject, but Lila was persistent.

"My wife can't have children."

"Oh, I'm sorry about that. You could always adopt."

"Yeah, I guess, but Angie doesn't want to do that." There was a knock at the front door.

"Oh. Hey the food is here. Put the movie on pause. I'll be right back."

"Wait a minute, birthday girl. I'm paying." Andrew pulled out a twenty and gave it to Lila. He then wiped the table off with one of the wipes they kept in the cabinet and took his jacket off. He could smell Nate's succulent ribs just before she walked back into the room.

"Good, you took that jacket off. Now you can really get down with these ribs."

"Aren't you afraid you're going to get something on that pretty dress?"

"You're right. I'll be right back." She raced into the bathroom, fumbled through her backpack for the bell-bottom jeans and halter she had worn to the photographers, and changed. When she returned, she pushed play on the VCR and sat at the small table. "Okay. Let's dig in."

Andrew wasn't sure if he wanted her to wear the dress or the outfit she had on now. At least her stomach wasn't showing when she was wearing the dress. Now he could see more than he needed to. She was apparently oblivious to what she was doing to him. All the young girls were wearing body-baring outfits these days anyway, and Andrew assumed her wardrobe was merely a reflection of fashion and not intent on her part. They ate and laughed as they watched the movie. He couldn't remember when he'd had such a good time. Lila was young, but she was also funny and uncomplicated. Whatever she felt she said without hesitation. As they watched the movie, they talked as if they were old friends.

"Thank you for the birthday party, Mayor."

"You are most welcome. Now, do you need a ride home? I better get back to my speech, and you better get back home before Barb starts to worry."

"She'll be okay, but I could use a ride home. I think the bus stopped running already. The first thing you need to work on when you become mayor is public transportation. It sucks in this town."

"I will look into that, my dear. Now, your chariot awaits." Andrew put his jacket back on and waited while Lila got her backpack.

"I know you're going back to the office when you drop me off," Lila said as she slid into the passenger side of his jeep.

"You're right. I have a lot to do if I want to win this election."

"You already won. Nobody wants that old coot who has been running this town into the ground for the last few years."

"Aren't you too young to be interested in this kind of stuff?"

"I've always liked politics, and of course I live with my Auntie Barb, who talks about local politics all the time. She got me interested in this election. Besides, age is just a number, as they say."

"Okay, you win." It did not take long to drive the short distance to her aunt's, and Andrew pulled in front of Barbara's apartment and waited while Lila got her things.

"Thanks again," Lila said before she got out of the Jeep. Andrew nodded his head and waited for her to open the apartment door.

"No. Thank you," he said softly after she was safely inside. He pulled back onto the main street with a heavy heart. Lila had reminded him of how lonely he had been the last year. Angie had so many functions and benefits to attend that he couldn't keep up with them. She was presently in Chicago visiting her sick aunt and wouldn't be back for another week. He pushed their little adventure out of his head and tried to concentrate on his upcoming battle with the great Douglas Kennedy. Mister Kennedy had plenty of cash and the incumbency in his favor. Andrew would have to rely on the people's desire for change to win this one.

CHAPTER 3

The people of Juniper were indeed ready for change, and they proved it by electing Andrew Blake handily. Angie was ecstatic and floated around the house as if she were royalty. She initiated sex with him on several occasions, which she hadn't done since they were newly married, but not long after, Andrew's mission completed, Angie reverted to her old self. Andrew kept his promise to Lila and managed to get her hired on as a clerk, which almost took an act of God. Most of the staff had been in their jobs for years and did not like the idea of a young girl coming on board, especially one so attractive as Lila. Andrew made sure her resume got to the right people, however, and when they read that Barbara was not only a reference but her aunt, Lila was welcomed into the fold.

One night, Andrew was working late and Angie was on one of her shopping excursions to the mall or wherever. Lila had not seen Andrew since she was selected for the job. She walked the long hall to his office and knocked on the door. There was a light but no one answered. She peered into the office and saw Andrew deep in concentration in front of his computer. She opened the door and stepped inside.

"Always burning the midnight oil, huh?" Lila said, now perching on his desk the way she had the night they shared ribs and a movie.

"You know me. I didn't hear you come in," Andrew replied, now studying the young woman before him. She had on a navy blue suit that hugged her as if someone had made it just for her. Her hair was pulled into a ponytail, and she wore wire-framed glasses, giving her that preppy look. She was as gorgeous as that first night he found it difficult to avoid staring at her cleavage or her bare stomach, but without revealing a thing.

"No, I don't know you, Andrew." That was the first time she had called him by his first name. She usually just called him Mayor. He cleared his throat and nervously brushed some imaginary lint off of his pants.

"Excuse me," Andrew said, trying to smile. She was making him nervous, and he didn't know why. They had always been able to talk, long after that first night in the campaign office, but tonight was different. The tension was so thick in the room you could cut it with a knife.

"No, I don't know you. I know His Honor, Mayor Blake, but not Andrew, the man behind the title. But I am here because I haven't even been able to thank you since you got me this job."

"Well, I've been too busy to find you, but you deserved the promotion to paid status anyway."

"Yeah, right. You were trying to avoid me." She laughed and crossed her legs, watching his expression.

"Now, why would I want to avoid my favorite employee?"

"That's what I asked myself, and then it hit me. You're afraid of me. You think I might be one of those freaks looking for a free ride and possibly a blabber mouth who would spread it all over town if something were to happen between us."

"Whoa there, young lady. Nothing ever happened between us." Andrew got up and peered out into the hallway to make sure no one was within earshot of their conversation then closed the door.

"Relax. The building is empty. I checked before I walked down here. I took the bus, so your car is the only one in the parking lot besides the one the security guard drives."

"You are something else, you know that? You should be running around with some young brothers your own age."

"I don't baby sit." My aunt can take care of the boys my age. Her boyfriend is only thirty-eight." Andrew's look of surprise made her giggle.

"What!" Andrew said, truly surprised.

"Yes. Old Barb loves the young ones, and they love her back. She really doesn't look her age, you know."

"So what do you like, Lila?" Andrew asked peering over his reading glasses.

She hesitated before she spoke. "I like you."

"You don't want an old married man, Lila. You're too special to waste your time being the other woman."

"You think I'm special?"

"Yes, and you're a beautiful girl."

"Woman, Andrew. I thought I told you that girls go to public school."

He smiled. "That's right, you did. Forgive me..."

Lila stepped in front of him and pressed her lips to Andrew's. He pushed his tongue into her mouth and tasted her sweetness. She gasped as his hand went under her shirt. His fingers brushed her breast, sending chills up her spine.

Before he knew it, they were locked in an embrace. There was no turning back now. Andrew had done everything in his power not to end up in this position, but lust would have its reward tonight. Lila's body was beckoning to him like a fox to a hound. They moved together like dancers, as if their union had been choreographed. Andrew's hands were every where, and Lila held on for dear life. She needed someone to love her now. She had waited long enough. They collapsed onto the couch with a thud.

When they were finished, Lila went into the bathroom to freshen up and get back into her clothes. Andrew stood outside the door. "Where do we go from here, Miss Lila?" he asked, pushing the door to the bathroom open just a little so he could hear her response.

"Wherever you want to go, Andrew. When you decide, you just let me know. I'm going to slip out the back door and catch the last bus. You still haven't done anything about prolonging the hours that public transportation is available, so I have to hurry. Call me when you know where we're going. She left the bathroom, brushed by him, and slipped out of the door before he could object. He didn't notice the small package until she had gone. He opened the gift box and pulled out a small snow globe of the city. He shook it up, and watched as the snowflakes fluttered to the bottom. He knew where they were going from here, but he didn't know where they'd ultimately end up.

CHAPTER 4

Andrew and Angela Blake were on the front page of the *Desert Den*. The caption under their picture stated that they were celebrating ten years of wedded bliss. Angela was smiling and flashing the diamond her husband had presented to her, and Andrew stood stoically by her side. He neither laughed nor smiled but looked like a bystander who had accidentally walked into the photo.

Lila read the article that covered the marriage from the beginning to the present. She had been invited to the celebration along with all the other people in the building, but she had begged off, saying she would be out of town for a while. She threw the paper down and got up to get dressed. It hurt to see Andrew's wife parading around in the news, and to see her parading around town with Andrew, when Lila was the one keeping him happy.

The jealous feeling didn't last long. She was the one Andrew was flying to Kansas for a lovers' getaway. He had inherited some land from his grandfather and wanted to take a look at it. Angie refused to leave so close to the annual Thanksgiving dinner that Juniper financed for the homeless community, one of her obligations as the town's first lady.

Every year, community leaders planned a Thanksgiving meal and charged a hefty fee per plate. The proceeds from the fundraiser were then donated to the local homeless shelter for supplies and other necessities needed throughout the year. It was always a big success, and Angie thrived on the attention she received as the chairperson.

Lila concocted a story about her aunt being sick and needing to care for her, and her supervisor was nice enough to offer to drive her to the airport, which she declined. She assured her that she would be able to take a taxi without maxing out her funds. What her supervisor didn't know was that Lila could take a taxi to the next town and not put a damper on her funds.

Lila knew the trip they were planning was wrong, but she couldn't change her mind now. She and Andrew had a lot of fun together, and they liked the same things. Many of the girls from her graduating class had babies, and they had no good men lying around their apartments waiting for the next month's supply of food stamps. She visibly shivered when the thought crossed her mind. Whatever the downside to sleeping with a married man who happened to be the mayor, at least she knew that would not be her fate.

Lila had only told a partial lie. Barbara had recently moved to St. Louis with her new husband, and Lila was looking forward to visiting with her for a few days. The letters her aunt sent indicated that she was doing well and didn't have to work, but Barbara was still trying to play matchmaker and had hinted at inviting a friend for dinner when Lila arrived. Lila couldn't tell her about Andrew, and so she went along with the arrangement to keep the peace. Aunt Barbara told her she'd be pleasantly surprised. Lila figured he'd be a carbon copy of Leonard, Barbara's husband, with his cornrows and ghetto swagger.

Andrew had booked her in a separate hotel, erring on the side of caution. David, Andrew's close friend and someone she had heard about but never met, was in town with him. She had a feeling David already knew about her, but she wasn't concerned. Andrew had told her that he and David went way back and that whatever they knew about each other remained between the two of them.

Lila finished placing her things into the suitcase and changed the message on her answering machine. She forwarded her messages to her cell phone and turned off everything in the apartment. She looked around one last time and was grateful for all that she had accomplished in the last year. She had purchased her own furniture with money her aunt had saved in an account for her, and Lila had scrimped and saved the rest of the money she needed by budgeting and being careful. Her friend Dayna had come down to visit from college and had teased her about being so frugal. She just smiled and ignored her comments. Dayna had no idea where she had come from and how hard she would fight not to ever go back.

CHAPTER 5

The taxi driver honked the horn and hung his head out of the window to look for his passenger. Lila grabbed her bags and headed out the front door, locking it behind her. She waved at the driver to let him know she was on her way. She had forgotten to check the mail, and she ran to the box and collected the mail before jumping into the back of the taxi as the driver put her bag in the trunk. The driver mumbled something as he flicked on the meter and they sped out of the apartment complex parking lot. Sandra flipped through the bills and stopped when she got to a pink envelope. Her name and address were typed neatly in the center. She inhaled the floral scent from the envelope and slid her manicured nail along the inside of the envelope to inspect its contents: "I can't wait to see you again. Sincerely, A."

Lila smiled as she folded the envelope and placed it inside her purse along with the other mail. She could hardly wait either. She would endure her aunt's matchmaking only because she didn't want her digging into her business, and then she and Andrew could have two wonderful days together without Angie. Lila was leaving sunshine and warm days behind and heading for real winter, but she had Andrew to keep her warm in Kansas.

The taxi driver was going a lot faster than the speed limit as they made their way to the airport. Lila had always heard the cabbies were more likely to take their time so the fare would be higher, but she reasoned that maybe this guy had somewhere else to be.

When Lila saw the airport on the horizon, her heart began to beat wildly. She couldn't believe she was actually getting away from Juniper on a plane. This was her first time flying, and she couldn't wait to get aboard the jet. She was still thinking about Andrew, however. Maybe after this week with her, he would finally see that she should be on his arm and not Angie. Lila pulled out her wallet and paid the taxi driver, tipping him ten dollars.

"Thank you lady," he said, smiling greedily. She smiled in return as she slid out of the taxi. Finally, she had time with her man. She was feeling very special today. How many nineteen-year-olds could say they had a good job and an influential man flying them to a private getaway? "Not many," she thought to herself. She was on her way up and never wanted to see the bottom again.

She decided some time ago that her mother had done her a favor by leaving her behind. She would have probably dropped out of school and taken a minimum wage job if her mother had not left her with Aunt Barbara, but instead, Lila had been fortunate to leave their small town and start a new life. She didn't know where her mother was and she didn't care. She just thanked God that she didn't have to live in the house with a bunch of junkies ever again. She made her way through the airport check-in like an old pro, closed her eyes as soon as the seatbelt light went off, and didn't wake up until the plane landed.

Baggage claim was full of people trying to get somewhere for the holiday season. It was still a week before Thanksgiving, but from the crowded airport you would have thought it was closer. She had almost missed getting a ticket because of the holiday traffic, but Andrew had found one at the last minute. Lila went to the baggage claim and retrieved her luggage and sat down to wait for her aunt. She hoped Barbara wouldn't bring the man she was setting her up with to the airport. She wasn't in the mood for chitchat with a stranger.

She could see the snow falling outside the terminal window and pulled her short leather coat a little tighter. She wasn't used to such winters. If snow fell in Juniper, which it did only on rare occasion, it melted within the hour.

"Hel-lo-oh. You wanna give your old aunt a hug?" Barbara said standing over Lila with arms outstretched. Lila had been looking the other way and did not see her approach.

"Hey Auntie, I missed you. You look good. I guess married life agrees with you."

"It does. You ought to try it," Barbara said, winking at Lila.

"Don't start, lady."

Barbara grabbed one of Lila's bags and cackled at her independent niece. "Leonard has the car double parked outside. He's too cheap to pay for parking. We need to get a move on so he doesn't get a ticket." They rushed through the terminal and out into the street where Leonard had just made a turn and was on his way back to the front of the terminal.

"What's up, girl?" Leonard hollered in his aggravatingly whiny voice.

"Hello Leonard," Lila said dryly. She had never liked Leonard, but he was good to her aunt, and that was enough to make her cordial to him.

"Still stuck on yo'self, I see. Ain't nobody putting up with that in K-town. This here is where the real dogs get down."

"Whoop, whoop," Lila said sarcastically, praying he would talk to his wife and leave her alone. Barbara just laughed and told her husband to shut up.

"Don't pay Leonard no mind, Lila. He's full of himself today. He got promoted and is second to the man in charge, which means he has a steady income as long as he wants. Wait 'til you see our house. Leonard remodeled it himself. He has a lot of talent." There was much pride in her tone. "Now aren't you glad you came to visit and didn't have to sit in that boring town by yourself?" Barbara said, turning to look at Lila.

"Yes, I am. I can't wait to see your house, Auntie." She really was glad to see her aunt, the woman who had taken her in and cared for her without asking anything in return. Her own mother hadn't cared for her nearly as well.

"You're in for a treat. Samuel, that's Leonard's friend, is coming about six. He's in contracting too."

Leonard turned off the main street onto a bricked-in area called Westlake. All the houses were large and had beautiful manicured lawns just like the ones she'd seen in the housekeeping magazines. Leonard opened the four-car garage of one of the massive homes and pulled in. Lila saw her aunt's blue Camero on the other side of the garage, which was immaculate. Shelves lined the walls of the garage and boxes were placed neatly on each shelf. An upright toolbox stood on the right side of the shelves, each tool neatly in place.

"It's better inside. Come on," Barbara said, closing the garage door. She was right. A huge fireplace with brown stucco accents faced the door they entered. The carpet in the living room was a cream color, and it was filled with white leather furniture and beige throw pillows. Lila could have put the contents of her whole apartment in that one room. The white marble-topped table in front of the large sofa had an arrangement of white roses, and a statue of a woman in cream-colored garments with a basket on her shoulder stood on one side of the sofa.

"This is beautiful," Lila exclaimed, spinning around to soak in the room. Barbara just smiled and clapped her hands to turn on the lights.

"You've only seen one room, chick. Come on into the kitchen, which is my pride and joy," Barbara said as she led the way. Lila could not believe her eyes. The craftsmanship that had gone into making the cabinets was truly impressive. There was an island in the middle of the kitchen with a rack of copper pots hanging over it just like she had seen in the housekeeping magazines. The kitchen was so big there was a futon in one corner and a television mounted on the wall in front of it.

Lila wanted to hang up her coat and cook something. One day, she decided, she wanted to have a home just like her aunt's.

"I didn't know you had it like this, Auntie." Leonard rolled his eyes at her on his way up the stairs with her bags.

"Leonard made the renovations to the house. I'll show you what we started out with later. I took pictures. He still has some work to do though. You want me to show you to your room or are you going to sleep in the kitchen?" Barbara said, laughing.

"Yeah, I better get some rest, but I want to cook something in this kitchen before I leave."

"You can fix us something when Leonard goes to work in the morning. He will probably hang out with the boys tomorrow since you're here."

"Hey, where's the fridge?" Lila asked, looking around the kitchen. Barbara stepped up to one of the cabinets beside the stove and opened it.

"Here it is. I was wondering when you were going to ask. Everybody does."

"Okay, this house is the bomb. Tell Leonard I'll hire him when I make my first mil," Lila said, now trailing wide eyed behind her aunt.

Barbara showed her around the rest of the house before she took her to the room where she would be staying. She felt as if she was being entertained by royalty. Her aunt had hit the jackpot with her young stud. The last four duds couldn't even buy a bus pass. Lila had lectured her aunt each time, but all her talking was in vain. Each man prior to Leonard had left under mysterious circumstances. Lila had always suspected that they had other women and just used her aunt for the money she gave them so freely.

Her mother and her aunt had been cut from the same cloth. They would do anything for a man. The only difference between her mother and her aunt was that her aunt didn't let anyone come between the two of them.

Barbara loved Lila's Cajun steak and eggs, and she said she'd be in the kitchen taking out steaks for breakfast. Barbara also told her they were going to a restaurant in town in two hours and she needed to find something to wear. It was freezing in Kansas, and Lila was glad she had purchased a few warm things for this trip or she would have frozen to death while she was here. The short leather jacket she had on was not enough, even though she had on a pair of cords and a turtleneck bodysuit. "Two weeks will be enough in this kind of weather," she thought as she unpacked her clothes.

CHAPTER 6

Samuel showed up at six, and as her aunt had predicted, Lila was pleasantly surprised when she walked into the room. He was fine and didn't talk in ghetto English. She couldn't believe Leonard could hold a conversation with Samuel, let alone call him friend. It must be true what they say, she thought: opposites do attract.

They had a good time at the restaurant, and after their dinner they stopped at a popular club in town to listen to some live jazz. Lila could see the ladies checking Samuel out, and she definitely understood why. Leonard swaggered around the club "talking loud and saying nothing," while her aunt sat at the table with them and chattered. She seemed to be used to Leonard's behavior and waved her hand when Lila asked if he was going to come back to the table.

"Leonard has to be seen, girl. I ain't thinking 'bout all that. He pays the cost to be the boss."

"Whatever," Lila said under her breath.

"I heard that, miss. Don't forget which of us is the aunt and which is the niece." Barbara laughed. My niece is fine, huh Samuel?"

"Fine's not even the word to describe this little beauty. They don't make 'em like this in Kansas City, Missouri, where I come from," Samuel said, smiling broadly.

"Oh, I'm sure there are some beauties around," Lila said.

"I didn't meet any. That's why I came to Kansas City, Kansas. I was looking for my soul mate. I think I can stop searching now," Samuel said as he winked at Lila.

"A love connection! I knew you two would hit it off," Barbara said, smiling at the two of them.

"Auntie, this is a first date. Nobody is in love. It don't work like that for me."

"Oh please, girl. You know you like Samuel. Ya'll young girls play too many games."

"I can wait, Barb. Don't push her. I have all the time in the world. After all, this is the first date, just as Lila said. Maybe the second date is the charm." Leonard came back to the table and sat down, toppling one of the chairs behind him. It seemed to Lila like wherever he went there was chaos.

"So, miss freeze. How you likin' Samuel. Didn't think I had any friends with class, huh?"

"I underestimated you, Leonard," she hissed, rolling her eyes at him. Leonard called her a name, but Samuel was asking her to dance and she missed what he said.

"You and Leonard don't get along, do you?" Samuel asked. She noticed that he towered over her. The brother was not only fine, but he was at least six foot five.

"He's a loud wanna-be. He wants to be more than he really is, but my aunt likes him, so I guess I can put up with him once a year."

"So you got somebody special in your life right now?"

Lila had to think before she spoke. Andrew was special, but she couldn't talk about that and so she chose her words carefully. "No. Not really."

"So, I do have a chance."

"Yes, you do. I'm enjoying myself, Samuel."

"Good. Maybe I can convince you to move to Kansas."

"Or maybe I can convince you to move to California," she said sweetly.

"You probably could, beautiful. You probably could."

She had no intention of letting a relationship with Samuel get too far. She would take his picture to work and talk of him often. She would even give him her work number, but her heart was off limits. She just needed someone to take away the loneliness when Andrew had to go back to his wife. She was glad she had come to Kansas. Her aunt had supplied her with the perfect cover.

CHAPTER 7

Angela twirled around before the mirror to get a second look at her reflection. She had shined brighter than every woman at the party in her black velvet dress that hugged every curve of her body. Even Andrew had to do a double take, and he lived with her every day. Most importantly, Josh sat at the back table and glared at her all evening. She knew he wanted her to divorce Andrew and follow him to some godforsaken place in the hills and raise babies, but that was not going to happen.

Josh was a tiger in bed, but he lost his appeal outside of the covers. She had finally drawn the attention of the one man she had wanted ever since she first met him. Andrew's best friend seemed uninterested until lately. It would take a while to have him in the way she wanted him, but he was worth the wait. She'd figure out what to do with Josh when the time came.

"Angie," Andrew called from the family room. She pranced down the steps and into the room behind him.

"You looking for me?"

"Did you have to wear that dress? You left nothing to the imagination tonight. What's wrong, not enough attention lately?" Andrew said, slamming his keys down on the coffee table.

"Oh, is the mayor mad? Did I make the big man disappear tonight?" Angela said in a mocking tone. She turned to go upstairs, but Andrew snatched her back around.

"I put up with your little dramas, but there were some very important people at that party tonight."

Angie snatched her arm away from his grasp. "If I remember correctly, it was our anniversary party, not a publicity stunt. Or was I mistaken?"

"You've been in the political game long enough to know what the deal is, Angie! I need to present a powerful and solid front if I'm going to get to the governor's seat. You can't run around looking like a..."

"A what, stick-in-the-ass Blake? A whore? Is that what you wanted to say? Well, you're the only one that didn't approve of the dress. I got plenty of compliments. Don't be upset because I stole your thunder tonight, because all eyes were on me."

"Watch yourself, Angie. You want to get to the governor's mansion just as bad as I do. The voters were with you when you were playing the good wife. You make them angry, and they'll have your fine little ass for dinner. If you need more attention, parade yourself around the office like you usually do. I'm sure the guys down there would enjoy the show."

Andrew stormed out of the room and up the stairs. He was sick of her flaunting her body like some teen girl, and as if he wasn't in the room. He'd put up with her crap long enough. Then he thought of Lila waiting for him in Kansas, and his mood changed. Angie would soon be his ex-wife, but he had to play his cards right. He wanted Lila beside him, but he had to find a way to make that happen.

"You can sleep in the spare room tonight. I don't need no angry black man next to me in bed."

"My pleasure. Nothing happens in this room anyway," Andrew said. He had changed into a pair of shorts and a tee shirt and was packing his suitcase. He couldn't wait to leave. If he didn't have a meeting in two days, he would have left right after the party. All he could think about was Lila and how good she made him feel. She had taught him what real passion was all about. He'd done all he could do to mend his broken marriage, but nothing had worked because Angie didn't want any part of being a wife let alone a mother. She hadn't bothered to mention that she didn't want any children before they got married. He wasn't even sure she was telling the truth when she said her doctor informed her that she couldn't have children. She was protected by the privacy act, so he couldn't even ask the doctor if her story was true.

Angie changed into her pajamas and slipped into bed. She was glad he was leaving in three days. Josh could stay with her every night that he was gone. She could use the workout. Andrew had never really turned her on, but she had been eager to make a name for herself in the community and was willing to endure his clumsy fondling to get what she wanted. She had to practically show him what to do when they first had sex. She was so exhausted and frustrated when they finished that she made herself unavailable until she was ready to go through it with him again. He had finally caught on enough to get through, but he didn't have Josh's skills.

Josh hit all the right spots the very first night they were together. He had been teaching her how to use the machines in the gym and the proper way to lift weights, and they had a couple of drinks after her workout one night. They had been seeing each other ever since. She was careful with their meetings, and Josh was happy as long as he believed she was going to divorce Andrew and leave town with him.

PostPartum

She had no intention of leaving Andrew and all that they had built together. She would find a way to get rid of Josh in due time.

"You are right about that, player. Nothing happens in this room even when you manage to get it up. Now take your raggedy ass into the guestroom and leave me alone!" Andrew smiled as he gathered his suitcase and a few other things from his dresser. She could keep her legs closed forever. Lila was willing and able to fulfill his needs.

CHAPTER 8

"I had a good time, Andrew. You know how to wine and dine a woman. I hate to bring this up, but does your wife appreciate the kind of man she has?"

"Angela has her own agenda. I don't think she cares what kind of man I am as long as I pay the bills and provide her with the life she wants," Andrew said as he slid his arms out of his coat. Lila hung their coats up in the closet and turned on the television.

"You want something from room service?" Andrew asked.

"I'm still full from dinner. I just want something to drink. I'll get us something from the soda machine down the hall." Lila started for the door but Andrew stopped her.

"I forgot something. I'll be right back."

Lila sat on the couch and flipped through the channels until he came back. Andrew returned with two champagne glasses and a bottle of champagne. "Oh, you plan to get me drunk and seduce me now?" Lila asked, and then she laughed.

"No, but I neglected to tell you that I've put you in for a promotion."

"What!" Lila said, clapping her hands like a small child.

"Freda is retiring in two months, and I want to start training her replacement — you."

"What about Gladys? She's next in line for a promotion isn't she?" Gladys had been a clerk for at least two years. She was always talking about waiting for something to open so she could move up.

"Read the job description when you get back. You have to have skills, including typing at least sixty words a minute. Gladys can't take dictation, she's slow, and you know she can't type." We'll find something else for her to do," Andrew said. He twisted the cork and popped it off the bottle, then filled the glasses and made a toast.

"To my new community relations clerk. May we have many beautiful years together."

Lila smiled and clinked glasses with him. "You know you're serving alcohol to an underage person, Andrew."

"Are you going to turn me in?" Andrew asked, pulling Lila close to him. He sipped the champagne and pressed his mouth on hers to share the champagne. Lila then downed her champagne in one gulp. Andrew almost commented but changed his mind and filled the glasses again..

"So, are you happy about your new job, Miss Lila?"

Lila got up and set her drink down and went into the bedroom and came out with her CD player. "Let me show you how excited I am, Mister Mayor." She popped in the CD and *"I Get so Lonely"* flooded the room. Lila dimmed the lights stood in front of Andrew and began to strip to the music. Andrew sat back and enjoyed her unabashed seduction. She whirled her hips and bent over like a pro. He tried to get up and grab her, but she pushed him back down and continued to dance around him, getting close enough that he could touch her and then backing away. She was making him hungry for her with every move. He wasn't sure where she got her moves, but he would gladly pay the teacher for his or her time.

Andrew had a flashback to how his wife Angie had been in the beginning of their relationship. She had also blown his mind with her sexual prowess, but told himself that he couldn't have made the same mistake twice. Lila was nothing like Angie. She only wanted to please him and had never asked for anything in return. She had actually initiated their first encounter. No, this time he had won the prize. Now all he had to do was figure out how to keep her without compromising his new position or his future in politics. He knew that Angie could care less what he did, but the voters would not be so forgiving.

CHAPTER 9

"Hey, Joe. Is the mayor in his office yet? We have a small crisis over here," Gladys said as she scurried to her desk to pick up the note that she had just received from one of the curriers.

"Gladys, can you stop the dramatics and tell me what you're talking about," Joe said, trying not to get too caught up in Gladys' drama. He hoped this was one of the times she was acting because he had just edited and typed up the mayor's speech for the annual Thanksgiving event and wanted to enjoy a moment's peace.

Gladys had been working in the office a year by the time Joe joined the mayor's team. She had been really nice to him in the beginning, teaching him what people to avoid and other things that would make his job easy. She had even taken to calling him her adopted son. As soon as he was moved to a better paying position, Gladys conveniently forgot she ever knew Joe Fontano, and from then on, Gladys was a thorn in his side.

"The transportation guys are at it again. I got it from a reliable source that they are talking strike. Somebody better tell his majesty what's happening before he gets blindsided. "

Joe took the note that Gladys held out to him and read it. He recognized the source right away and knew this meant a strike was definitely going to happen. Their timing was perfect. They were getting ready for the annual winter benefit, and whoever planned the strike knew that half the city would need transportation to get to the biggest event of the season. Joe shook his head as he dialed Lila's extension. She picked up on the first ring.

"You better get down here right now. There's trouble in paradise."

Lila slammed the phone down and headed for Joe's desk. She knew he wouldn't call her down unless there was something important about to happen. "What's up, dude?" Lila asked as she perched on the side of Joe's Desk. They had a very good working relationship and were often seen out at lunch and dinner together. Joe had political aspirations of his own to pursue, and he was at least as dedicated to making sure that those aspirations were achieved as he was to assisting the mayor. He had made it plain to Lila and everyone else that this job was a stepping stone to greater things. Lila understood Joe and admired his honesty. He ignored the comments the females made about him when he turned down their advances. He knew what he wanted and didn't want any distractions in the workplace.

Lila and Joe had talked at length when she first started working for the mayor. They both shared the same hunger for success, and both had come from meager beginnings and vowed never to go there again. Unlike Lila, Joe was raised by both his parents, but they never had enough of anything. Joe told Lila about the times he had to go on the streets of Manhattan with his father to earn money. His father played guitar while little Joe monitored the money people dropped inside the guitar case. He was humiliated each time the coins clinked in the felt-lined bottom of the case, with every dollar bill that floated to rest there. His father could only keep his more legitimate gigs for two or three months at a time because of his drinking. His mother did the best she could with the meager earnings his father brought home.

Joe's father had left Juniper to make it in the big apple but lost everything instead. After one of his long drinking spells, a policeman had come to the house and informed them that his father was in the hospital and they needed to come quickly. Joe's mother wrapped his baby sister up and dragged them both down to the hospital he was born in on Fifth Avenue. His father never regained consciousness and died of cirrhosis of the liver.

His mother returned to Juniper and she and her kids lived with her parents until his mother found a job at the post office. Joe had maintained a 4.0 all the way through high school and won himself a scholarship to Cal State.

Lila read the note that Joe gave her and frowned. This was just what they needed, a protest just when the mayor was making some good points with the community because there were more jobs and there was more recreation for the kids since he took office. Lila knew the source was legitimate because Gladys' boyfriend had always given them good tips. He was honest and respected by everybody at city hall. He always seemed to know what was happening in town before anyone else because he had lived in Juniper all his life and had friends everywhere.

Lila took the note and knocked on Andrew's office door. They had to come up with a plan, and quick, to ward off the trouble headed their way. The benefit was on the thirtieth, which gave them three days to stall the issue or eliminate it altogether. Andrew was on a business call and couldn't be interrupted, but she hoped the phone call was quick so she could give him the news and help plan a strategy.

Lila had another reason for wanting to speak to Andrew — she missed him. They hadn't been together since their getaway in Kansas.

PostPartum

She knew she was getting too caught up in the relationship, especially since he was married, but she couldn't help herself. Andrew was her world. He just needed to move Angela out of his.

CHAPTER 10

Angie tossed a pillow that had fallen to the floor back on the bed. Their bedroom was her favorite place in the house. The furniture was cherry wood and the bedspread and drapes were antique white lace. The cherry-wood floor was covered by a hand braided rug that matched the bedspread. Angela had selected a burgundy velvet loveseat and recliner for the corner of the room by the large picture window. A bookcase filled with all her favorite authors stood by the fireplace, which faced the loveseat and chair. Whenever her world was crashing in around her, she could curl up on the loveseat with a good book and get lost for hours.

Angie knew she would be spending most of the evening in her favorite spot now that Andrew's parents were spending the weekend with them. Mister Blake was okay, but Alice Duane Blake was a stuck-up prude. She had never liked Angela, and she did not make it a secret. She had her heart set on Andrew marrying some dreary little snot who lived next door to them back in the day. The only reason she wanted Andrew to marry the troll was because her father was one of the wealthiest men in the community, the president of the bank and a longtime friend of the family.

Andrew's mother had called Angie an alley cat and said that she wasn't good enough for her son to her face. Angie had lashed back at Mrs. Blake with the things her precious son was doing to her in private, and Mrs. Blake had retaliated by slapping Angie hard across her face. Angie had vowed that one day she would make Mrs. Blake pay for that slap.

Angie walked into the bathroom and started her bathwater. She slid out of her clothes, pulled a bottle of champagne from the small bar inside her nightstand, and rummaged through the drawer to find a lighter for the candle she kept on the sink. She was feeling a little horny at the moment and would even welcome Andrew's clumsy pawing. The champagne added to her current mood. Besides, if Andrew was able to get some, he'd be much more pleasant at the dinner table.

Andrew had been behaving a little different around the house lately, now that she thought about it. He was humming and completing all the little chores she'd asked him to do. He'd even sent her a note with flowers while he was in Kansas. Maybe there was hope for them after all. Or maybe the champagne had started to work.

"ANGIE!" Andrew shouted through the fog of delirium she was in. She could hear footsteps in the hall but she didn't answer or move. Andrew stomped into the bathroom, ready to ask her why she had ignored him. He found his wife smiling and with her eyes closed as her rested on her bath pillow. Her breasts rose above the soapy water just enough to tease him. He was so absorbed in the scene that he forgot the reason he had come into the bathroom.

He kneeled down beside Angie and nibbled her ear, then moved quickly to her mouth. She opened her mouth and waited for him to fumble his way to her mouth. He surprised her by planting a kiss on her nose, then on her neck.

"Get in," Angie whispered without opening her eyes. Andrew stripped out off his clothes and slid into the tub. He would explain what was happening at the office later. He wanted to take the ride while Angie was offering. He couldn't believe how easy it was for her to beckon him back into her world. Her appeal was especially hard to grasp now that he and Lila were having regular sex. He had to admit that he was still attracted to his wife no matter how she treated him. Lila was beautiful and sexy, but Angie had his heart. He had tried many times to get her out of his system, but not even Lila's warm body had worked. He was hooked for life.

Angie and Andrew played in the water like two newlyweds, splashing each other and kissing as if for the first time. Champagne, candlelight, and desire were an intoxicating combination. They made love on the floor of their bathroom over and over. Andrew whispered promises in Angie's ear while she worked her magic on his body.

When they were finished, they got back into the soapy water to wash off their lovemaking. They only had an hour before Andrew's parents arrived. Angie wanted to check in on Gayle, the cook, to see if she needed anything. Andrew's parents were from Louisiana and loved the food from their heritage, and Gayle's gumbo was one of their favorites. Angie stared at her husband as if he was a stranger. She hadn't noticed how handsome he had become. His body hadn't started to sag like most of the older men she knew, and he didn't have a gut.

"What's going on, Angie? You want a new car or some money?" Andrew asked, sliding on his socks and shoes

"You promised me a lot of things in that bathroom. Do you remember what they were?" Angie asked, smiling slyly.

"You know you're wrong for settin' a brother up like that. You know my parents will be here any minute. Hurry up and get dressed," he said, sliding on his pants.

"Don't try and weasel your way out of your promise. I'll get dressed, but I'm not forgettin' what you promised, mister!"

Andrew threw a pillow at Angie and went to the guestroom to make sure it was ready. He hadn't felt this good in his home in a long time. This could be a new beginning, he thought.

CHAPTER 11

Lila finished putting her powder on and took one last look in the mirror. Joe had asked her to be his date for the benefit and she had accepted. They had a lot of fun together, and Joe was safe. Her hairdresser had wrapped her bang over her left eye and around her ear, and the rest was pinned into a French roll. She wore the pearls that Andrew had given her on their trip with matching earrings. The black strapless gown had eight round pearls around the bodice that matched her set perfectly. She put on her black fur wrap, grabbed her black velvet clutch bag, and waited for Joe to escort her to the car.

"You look marvelous," Joe said, scanning Lila from head to toe. She was perfect wife material for someone like him, someone who wanted to run for public office. His girlfriend Sarah was pretty enough, but she just had no interest in politics, or anything else for that matter. She lived for the beach and getting her nails done. The only reason he was still dating her was because she threatened to kill herself if he left her. He didn't need any drama at the moment. He had decided that, right after finals, Sarah was going to be history with or without a funeral, but in the meantime, he had to string her along until he earned his Masters.

"You look good too, Joe. Thanks for asking an old single lady out. Why didn't Sarah come with you?" she asked after he had closed her door and climbed into the driver's seat.

"Sarah is in Phoenix visiting her father for the holidays. I didn't want to mess with her family obligations," Joe said. In truth, he was glad she was gone. Her clinging was messing with his head. He promised himself he would not date another clingy, needy woman again. It was physically draining. He and Lila made small talk the rest of the way to the event.

All of the top city officials were already mingling with the crowd when they got there. They had arrived early to counteract any problems that might arise before the benefit. The transportation committee had postponed their strike pending talks with the mayor — Joe had negotiated a stay until after the holidays — but there were a million other things that could go wrong.

Lila caught Andrew's eye long enough for him to nod to acknowledge her presence, and then he turned to his family, who were trailing him like the Paparazzi. Lila was about to take her seat when she spotted a familiar face at the entrance of the banquet hall. The woman began to flail her arms around to get her attention.

"Oh God," Lila gasped. Her mother and her new boyfriend were waving at her to come over.

"Lila, you okay? You look like you saw a ghost," Joe said, touching her arm. Joe didn't know how true his words were. She had seen something more horrible than a ghost.

"I'm okay, Joe. I'll be right back." Lila moved through the room with urgency, angry at her mother for showing up after a year with not even a letter or phone call since she saw her last.

"What are you doing here?" Lila asked, ignoring the attendant at the door. All that mattered was getting her mother away from her new friends and her new life. She pulled her mother into a separate hall where no one could see them.

"You not gone hug yo mama? I missed you," her mother said as she made a fumbling attempt to give Lila a hug. Lila pushed her away, and so Betty introduced Lila to her new boyfriend, Craig, as if he was the king of the world. Craig grinned broadly, displaying four gold-plated teeth.

"Mother, I don't have time for a happy reunion. In about fifteen minutes we are going to start a benefit that helps homeless children. You remember what they are, don't you? I used to be one of them."

"You ain't never been no homeless child. We always had a place to lay our head."

"No, you always had a place, even if it was a crack house. I had to find my own place because your men couldn't keep their hands off me. Now, what do you want?" Lila asked glaring at her mother. She could not believe her mother would show up and try to ruin her happy event. At least she had the decency to have on clean clothes that fit. Craig must have been a little stricter about her attire than her previous lovers.

"Craig here just lost his job baby, and I hate to do it, but I need some money to tide us over. I ain't working right now because of my illness, and so we figured, since you doing so well, you could lend us a couple a dollars 'til we get on our feet." Betty's illness was her drug habit. All her life she heard about her mother's illness, but no one except for her aunt would admit that the illness was drug addiction.

"How much is a couple of dollars, Betty?" Lila asked, anxious to get them out of her sight.

"Just two hundred, the rent's paid and we paid our other bills, but we ain't got no free money. Craig here is going to pay you back soon as he get his first SSI check. He been approved already." Craig bobbed his head up and down and smiled as if someone had just told him he won the lottery.

"Wait here. When I come back, I'll have the money, and I want you two gone. Don't worry about paying it back, just leave." Lila knew she would never see the money again and she didn't care. Two hundred dollars was a small price to pay to get rid of her mother and this Craig. She rushed down the corridor to the front of the hotel where the teller machine was located. If she hurried, she could give them the money and slip back into the hall before everyone sat down for the opening.

Lila was back in a flash and watched in bitter amusement as her mother and Craig scampered down the hall into the night with their good fortune. Lila turned to go back inside and bumped into Joe.

"Who in the world was that, Lila? Joe asked.

"Oh, somebody I used to know. Come on. Let's go back inside. It's chilly out here." In her rush to get her mother out of sight again, Lila had forgotten her wrap. The hallways were a little cooler than the banquet hall. She tried to calm down and to continue with the evening in her previous festive mood as they took their seats. She couldn't help but think about her mother now, however. Betty had lost a lot of weight and looked like death walking. Craig was at least six foot three with a half-afro, half-perm. The ghetto "Bonnie and Clyde" hadn't bothered to say thank you. Lila shook herself as if to rid herself of the memory, and then she turned to her date for the night, but it was no use.

Joe whispered something about the speaker for the night, but Lila was far away again, back in the house where her mother had last left her. She could still feel the pain of coming home one day and being told her mother was gone and would be back soon. Days turned into weeks and weeks into months, but Betty didn't come back. Marcus, her unofficial guardian and her mother's boyfriend, had been good to her at first, buying her clothes and paying for all her school needs; but slowly Marcus began to require more of her.

He had used her fear of the dark to get her into his bed. Once she was in his bed, he slowly worked his way into molesting her. He would bring her something pretty, and then he'd ask for kisses and hugs. On her eleventh birthday, she began to have unprotected sex with a thirty-five year-old man almost every day of the week, and there was nothing anyone could do, or so she thought. He'd convinced her that, if she told, she would end up in a home for bad girls.

Lila didn't known it at the time, but her Aunt Barbara had been looking for her, and when she didn't get answers to the letters she sent, she drove out to Apple Valley to look for her niece. Her Aunt told her later that she figured her sister had lit out with someone and left the girl to fend for herself. Barbara had tried several times to get custody of Lila, but her sister was clever enough to move each time she got close.

Lila had just gotten home from school one day when she heard a knock at the door. Marcus wasn't home yet, and she opened the door to find her Aunt Barbara standing there with her arms crossed. Lila was so relieved to see her that she almost fell into her aunt's arms. Barbara told Lila to pack a bag and say good-bye to flopping from one place to another.

"I'm going to court for you. You don't ever have to worry about where you live again. A child needs a home where they feel safe. I don't know what's wrong with Betty that she can't see that, but I'm filing paperwork as soon as I get back to Juniper."

Lila was still clutching her aunt as she told her this, glad someone had finally come to rescue her. She couldn't find any words that would convey what she felt at that moment. Barbara squeezed her tightly and kissed the top of her head. Lila reluctantly let go of her aunt and went to get her things

"Who have you been staying with here, Lila?" Barbara asked flipping, through the small pile of mail on the table. Lila froze. She couldn't tell her aunt she was living with one of her mother's boyfriends, especially after what he'd been doing to her.

"I don't know who he is Auntie — let's just go." Lila had her diary and a few items her mother had bought her. She didn't want any of the clothes Marcus had purchased. They represented something she never wanted to feel again.

"Baby, what's wrong? I know you weren't living here by yourself." Her aunt stared at her, waiting for a response. Lila shifted from one foot to the other but words escaped her. "It's okay, baby. Let's go."

It took a while, but Lila finally told her aunt all that went on with Marcus. Barbara had no way of finding someone that only had a first name and no other identifying information, and apparently no one in the neighborhood had seen him up close because Barb asked. She had made Lila sit in the car while she went door to door asking if anyone had seen the man who lived in the corner apartment. No one had seen a thing. The animal had done his deed and ran back to hell where his kind waited until their next victim appeared. Lila was secretly glad they couldn't find Marcus. She wanted to forget he ever existed.

CHAPTER 12

Andrew dialed David's home number and waited for someone to answer. He prayed that David answered and not his wife, Jeanette. He hadn't spoken to her since high school, and he had no desire to talk to her now. Jeanette hated his guts, and he couldn't do a thing to change it. He had been dating her sister, Tina, in high school. Tina had gotten pregnant, but she didn't tell him. She simply disappeared for a while, and by the time he found out that she was pregnant, she'd had an abortion and was in the hospital. Five days later, Tina was dead. No one at school knew that' she was pregnant or what had really happened to her, but Andrew knew. She wrote him a letter and slid it into his locker the day she went to have the abortion. He still had the letter locked in his safe. Jeanette's mother and father said Tina died of a blood clot in her brain, and no one was ever the wiser, but he and Jeanette shared the secret. He knew that Tina's death wasn't his fault, but Jeanette blamed him anyway.

"Hello," David said, trying to wake up.

"Boy, how come you still in bed? Get up. I need you to come to my office for a few minutes," Andrew said.

"Andrew, it's seven o'clock on a Sunday morning. What are you doing in your office today?" David had eased out of bed and carried the receiver into the hallway so Jeanette could sleep.

"We need to talk, and I don't want people all around when we do it. Can you be down here in the next half hour?"

"Alright, man. Give me forty-five, but this better be good." David went back into the bedroom, eased the phone onto the base, and headed for the shower. He hoped Andrew wasn't in trouble. His life was going good at the moment. He peeked into the room to see if Jeanette was still sleeping. She usually slept until nine o'clock without waking. All he needed was to get out the door before she asked any questions. He'd come up with an excuse to be out and about so early on a Sunday later.

Andrew paced the office while he waited for David. He cleaned and sprayed the office so there would be no evidence of the sex that he just had with Lila. Angie had finally started to act like his wife, but he just couldn't give up Lila. He knew he was playing with fire, but he had no intentions of stopping his affair. But Lila was the least of his problems. Joe had phoned him at home to tell him that somebody on the transportation team had it in for him. Even though they had agreed to table talks until after the New Year, there was a rumor that someone was going to sabotage one of the bus routes. If anyone could find out what was going on, David could. He was a homeboy who had worked hard to make a good life for himself and his family with his trucking business.

Andrew's family had come to town when Andrew was in ninth grade. They had never really been accepted by the hardworking people of Juniper. The talk around town was that the Andrews thought too highly of themselves, and most people stayed away from them. It had taken a couple of years for them to finally be accepted into the community.

Andrew hadn't known it then, but his father was a successful business man and had always invested wisely. He'd learned that his father's father was a prominent white business mogul, and though Andrew never lived with the elder Mister Blake, he made sure his son had a healthy inheritance when he reached legal age.

There were plenty of secrets in their house during his youth, but Andrew was busy being "mister everything." Whatever he asked for simply seemed to always appear. Life was good then. The thought quickly faded as the problems at hand invaded his brain. He dreaded going into negotiations with the transportation guys. He knew one man had a grudge that he would not let go of. "Where is David?" he thought as he paced the floor.

David swaggered into the double doors with a cigarette hanging out of his mouth. He never came around when the office was open. David and Andrew had agreed that anonymity was best for their relationship. David towered over Andrew with his bulky six five, two-hundred pound body.

"'Bout time, boy. Come in and sit down. I need some real good detective work on this one. Joe found out that, even though we discussed letting the transportation matter go until the holiday season was over, someone is still trying to sabotage the system. One of our riders found a pile of dog crap next to a sign that said, 'This is what the Mayor thinks of you.' Now you know James is one of the drivers who always has some issues, and you know why. I can't say that it's him for sure, but you know James," Andrew said from behind his desk.

"You think that James is still holding a grudge because Angie dumped him in high school? Come on Andrew, the brother had to grow just a little," David said, shaking his head.

"I didn't tell you this before because Angie begged me not to, but when Angie and I first got married, James would drive by our place and park up the street where the candy store was and stare down at our place. One day he got drunk and caught Angie on her way out and tried to get her to go away with him. She came back in the house hysterical. I tried to go out and get his sorry behind, but he was gone by the time I got outside."

"Man, I thought James had more on the ball than that," David muttered, scratching his head.

"What I need is for you to keep your ear to the ground. Find out what is going on with these guys and why. I'm more than willing to listen to their complaints, but I have to make a decision for the raise based on the budget. You know that. When you find out something, call me or come see me directly. I'm not sure who my enemies are anymore."

CHAPTER 13

Lila woke up at six a.m., two hours before she wanted to get up. She took the remote from the nightstand, flicked on the television, and started channel surfing. If she could find a good movie, it would help her go back to sleep. The phone rang before she finished her search.

"Who is calling me this early," Lila said as she reached for the phone. She checked caller ID and saw Samuel Payton on the display. She clicked the phone on.

"Samuel, do you know what time it is?" Lila said, but she also had to wonder if something was wrong with her aunt.

"Hello, gorgeous. I thought you might want to talk to a friend this morning. You were on my mind, and so I called. Should I call back later?"

"Uh no. We can talk. I was tossing and turning anyway. So what's up, Samuel?"

"Well, I'll be up in about four hours. My sister talked me into coming to her house for a few days, and I thought I'd fly into Juniper, pick you up, and take you with me."

"How am I going to go to your sister's house? She doesn't know me. I don't want to impose like that." Lila hated being in a place where she felt uncomfortable.

"Crystal and Jade would be happy to meet you. Don't knock something you've never tried.

"Who is Jade?"

"My seven year-old niece, Are you afraid of kids?" Samuel asked, smiling to himself. He remembered how Lila had watched a little girl playing with a doll at the restaurant, how her eyes filled with joy, but he hadn't mentioned it.

"I like kids. I just don't know," Lila said hesitantly.

"Well, if you don't like the visit, I'll return you to Juniper and go back by myself. Come on now, don't make me beg," Samuel pleaded into the phone.

"Okaaaay! I better not get down there and find out there's no sister and niece and it's a booty call."

"You don't know me well yet. You'll find out that I don't do the booty call play. See you in about four hours. Oh, and I'm renting a car. Just give me directions to your place, and please woman, be ready."

Lila hung up the phone and jumped out of bed. She was excited about seeing Samuel again. There was something calming about him, but she couldn't put her finger on what it was about him that made her feel that way. She tried on at least ten outfits before she settled on a cream cashmere sweater and a pair of matching cords. She dug through her shoe boxes looking for her cream-colored short boots like a mad woman.

Lila had never been to San Diego, and so she wasn't sure about the weather. She packed warm clothes and jackets to go with her other outfits. She raced around the house picking up things and cleaning as if her apartment wasn't already clean. She prided herself in keeping her place immaculate. She showered, put on her underwear, and lay back down to take a nap before Samuel showed up.

The room grew dark, and she could hear the familiar sounds of the same dream. Marcus came in with a box of candy, and she could hear herself in the dream begging him to go away. His figure loomed over her but she never saw his face. She only saw his shadow and heard his voice as he told her what to do. She cried and tried to leave the room, but Marcus's shadow blocked the door. She felt herself crying and pulling the covers over her head, but she didn't hear the door, not at first. Samuel was ringing the bell and pounding on the front door.

Lila sat straight up in the bed and looked around. She had to make sure the shadows had gone before she got out from under the covers. Her body was covered in sweat and her heart was racing — she had to remind herself that it was just a dream. She jumped when Samuel started to knock again.

"Just a minute," she called as she looked around frantically for her robe. She flattened her hair down and rushed to the door.

"Who is it?" Lila asked, trying to get herself together.

"Samuel. You know, the one you agreed to go to San Diego with."

Lila opened the door and let Samuel in. She hadn't realized that the lights were not on, but she was glad he couldn't see her face. Samuel stepped in and looked around. It was nearly eleven o'clock and now quite light outside, but it was dark inside her apartment.

"Is there something wrong, Lila?" Samuel said softly. Lila turned her back to Samuel and dried her eyes.

"No. I fell asleep after you called and just woke up. Turn the light on over there and I'll be right back."

Lila went into the bedroom to get herself ready. She normally had a little time to get herself together after one of her dreams. Usually, the dreams came to her during the night when she was at home alone. She washed her face, brushed her teeth, and put on the clothes she had laid out for herself. She pulled her suitcase out into the living room.

"Well I'm ready. I hope you don't mind stopping to get something to eat. I'm starving."

"No problem. Lila, is everything okay. I know you said you just woke up, but you looked as if someone had scared you."

"Just a bad dream, I'm fine now. Let's go." Samuel followed Lila out and watched while she locked her door. He was sorry she hadn't felt comfortable enough to tell him what was going on yet, but he knew she would in time.

Samuel had rented a red corvette. He put her luggage in the trunk alongside his luggage and opened the door for her. She was glad he at least had manners. Andrew had gotten so used to her now that he just called when he wanted to have sex.

"So talk to me. How's life in politics?" Samuel asked once they were on the road.

"It's okay, I guess, but I'm not really in politics. I'm just a community affairs clerk. Typing, filing, and bringing coffee is my life right now, but I'm not complaining. I feel blessed to have all of the things I have."

"So you do acknowledge that it is a blessing to be doing well, huh?" Samuel asked, looking at Lila.

"Yes I do. For whatever reason, God has decided to help me, even though I don't deserve it. God has a lot of patience if He would help someone like me, believe me."

"You are so right. God is infinitely patient. None of us deserves his grace, but he gives it anyway. I'm just glad he smiles down on a brotha like me," Samuel said, smiling.

"Okay Samuel, tell me about your sister and her little girl."

CHAPTER 14

"Jade is living in Navy quarters in San Diego. Her husband is in Iraq right now on a ship, and Crystal is their only child. I check on them once every six months or so. I promised my sister when her husband left that I would make sure Crystal had a man's influence in her life. I'm a little late with this visit. I was supposed to come last month, but I got caught up at work."

"It's nice of you to look after your family. Not many men do that."

"I'm not many men. Where do you want to eat? The lobster house is coming up, or we can wait 'til we get to San Bernardino and go to "Steak and Stein".

"I'll take steak," Lila said, smiling.

Samuel smiled as he looked at her beautiful face. He hadn't really been on a date in about a year. In fact, now that he thought about it, this might not be a date at all, but he felt like it was the beginning of something good.

"Okay, why are you smiling?" Lila asked.

"Just thinking about how sweet you look sitting over there smiling. You really know how to hook a man. I couldn't stop thinking about you after you left Kansas."

"You didn't call until this morning, so I must not have made too much of an impression on you."

"That's not true. You made a big impression. You have your career going and you are so confident. I just felt like you weren't being sincere when I asked you if you were seeing someone."

Lila was caught off-guard by his observation. She wiggled around in the seat so she could face the window. She couldn't tell Samuel that she was dating a married man, and she knew it, but nevertheless, something about the way he told her how he felt without any condemnation made her want to tell him. She stopped herself. She couldn't believe she was actually considering telling him about Andrew.

"Samuel, I am seeing someone. I just don't know if I'll keep seeing him. I wasn't sure how far our relationship was going to go. I mean, I really thought I cared about him, but the more I think about it, the more I see that he was just someone I was impressed with and who kept me from being lonely."

"How could a pretty young thing like you be lonely? I know men are falling all over themselves for you."

"Not the right ones," Lila mumbled.

"Well, I don't know who's right or wrong, but I'm falling. I just don't want to complicate things for you, so this trip will just be two friends going to San Diego for a little R and R, okay?" Lila felt so relieved at how understanding he was being that she nearly sighed aloud.

They stopped at the "Steak and Stein" and had dinner, and Lila was enjoying talking to Samuel about his childhood and his little niece. Some things made her wish that she had some fun things to share, but there weren't many things she even felt comfortable telling him. She remembered how happy she and her mother were when her grandfather was alive, but after he died her mother had turned to drugs and men to satisfy her needs and Lila was left to fend for herself.

Lila was now beginning to get a little excited about going to Samuel's sister's home. This was the first time someone had actually offered to take her to meet a family member. She certainly couldn't meet any of Andrew's family. Maybe she needed to change her rules to include finding happiness for herself, she thought. It wasn't New Years but she made a new resolution anyway — she was going to let down her guard and look for some real happiness.

CHAPTER 15

Navy quarters reminded her of upgraded projects. Samuel's sister's home looked exactly like the house next to it, and the one next to that. The only difference between these houses and projects was that the grounds were better kept and the buildings were much larger. She would have rather met his sister before coming to spend a weekend, but she kept reminding herself of Samuel's promise to take her home if she wasn't enjoying herself and tried to relax. Samuel had opened the trunk and removed their suitcases. "Here goes nothing," she mumbled to herself as she followed Samuel to the front door. Samuel rang the doorbell, turned to her, and winked.

"Uncle Sammie." A pretty brown little girl with curly puffs on each side of her head screeched and jumped into Samuel's arms. Lila smiled as the girl planted kisses on her uncle's forehead. When Samuel put his niece down, the girl turned and looked at Lila.

"Who's that?" she asked, pointing at Lila.

Samuel took his niece's hand and turned to Lila. "Lila, this is my favorite niece, Jade. Jade, this is a good friend of mine. Her name is Lila," Samuel said, smiling. Jade let go of her uncle's hand and walked right up to Lila.

"Hi, Lila. You're pretty. Is that all your hair?" Jade asked seriously. Lila laughed a little before answering her.

"Well, hello to you Jade, and yes, this is my hair."

A chocolate-colored woman with bronze twists and a big white smile entered the doorway. Lila knew by looking at her face that she was Crystal. She looked exactly like Samuel. Lila thought back to her childhood when her sister was living in the same town. No one knew that she and Lisa were related. Lila had long black silky hair and a fair complexion, but Lisa was very dark with long coarse hair. She'd heard the neighbors say that it was too bad Lisa hadn't inherited the hair, but Lila was always jealous of her sister's thick and pretty hair.

It'd been three years since she'd heard from Lisa. She missed her terribly, but they had never really been able to spend time together. Lisa's father hated their mother and refused to let his daughter mingle too much with her and Lila. He'd found a job in New York, uprooted his family and left. Her sister had confided that her father hated their mother and didn't want to end up in jail if he ran into her.

Lila never understood why Lisa's father took it out on her when she had nothing to do with what her mother had put him through. They wrote each other every week the first few years that Lisa was in New York. Then the letters came further and further apart until there was nothing coming at all. Lila knew it was because she and her mother were always moving from one address to another. As she looked into Crystal's face, she vowed to find Lisa as soon as she got back to Juniper.

"Lila, it's so nice to finally meet you. My brother has been going on and on about you ever since he met you in Kansas. I was beginning to think you were just a figment of his imagination. I'm glad you were able to visit with us." Crystal hugged Lila and led her into the house.

"Now, little miss nosy, will you show our guests where they will sleep while I finish the dishes and put out the cake I just baked? Can you guys eat dessert or are you full?"

"I can eat cake, Mommy," Jade said, motioning Lila to follow her up the stairs. Lila followed her little guide to the room where she would spend the weekend.

"You can put your clothes in those drawers. No one lives in this room. My uncle always sleeps downstairs, so he can protect us, Mommy says."

"Oh, it's nice to have protection. Your uncle is a nice man, huh?" Lila asked.

Jade bobbed her head up and down. "Yeah, and he's nice to everybody, even if you're not family. Do you have a lot of family, Lila?"

"Uh.... No, not really." Anxious to change the subject, Lila asked to see Jade's room. She did not want to think about her mother and all the hell she had put her through. Some things were best left behind, buried and untouched in the memory banks.

Lila followed Jade into her bedroom. When the little girl turned the light on, Lila felt like she was in another world. Jade's room was decorated with Barbie fashion. She had the curtains, bedspread set, and the rug. Her furniture was white with pink trim, and there was a white net over her toy chest, which was filled with stuffed animals, in the corner. Lila went to the Barbie house and looked inside. She remembered begging for a Barbie house when she was little, but her mother had other needs.

"You want to play Barbies?" Jade said excitedly. Lila nodded and sat down beside the house, awaiting instructions. Jade gave her two Barbies and a small pink box full of Barbie clothes. Jade selected two outfits and sat on the other side of the house and chattered on about them being friends and living together. Lila smiled and followed directions.

PostPartum

Jade was fun to play with. The grown woman and the little girl laughed
and played like two old friends.

CHAPTER 16

"Okay, little brother. You finally got her here. Now what? She is very pretty too. Those are the hard ones," Crystal said, and she laughed.

"I don't have plans. I just wanted her to meet you and Jade and get a feel for who I am. I'm not in a rush, Crystal. There is nothing I want more than to have Lila by my side, but she's obviously not ready," Samuel said.

"What are those two doing up there?" Crystal asked, now pausing to listen to the giggling. She tipped upstairs with Samuel behind her and peeked in on the two gigglers. Jade had her dolls outside the house on lounge chairs while Lila had her dolls at the kitchen sink in the house. They were so caught up in their game that they didn't notice Crystal and Samuel. Brother and sister crept back down the steps and into the kitchen.

"Samuel, she's a keeper. Did you see how she was playing with Jade? She isn't acting like she's too grown to play."

"Oh, so she's alright as long as she keeps Jade happy?"

"Shut up! You know I'm not that easy. I just think you have to be a special person to play with a little person you just met."

"You're right. I think Lila has shut herself off from a lot of things. I'm hoping this weekend will help her relax and enjoy new experiences."

"I told you to pursue that Psychology degree. You missed your calling."

"Lila, I like you. You really know how to play Barbies. Let's be best friends." Jade said, plopping her Barbie down and hugging Lila's neck.

"Let's do that then." Lila squeezed the little girl back and they shook hands to seal the deal. Lila tried not to, but she could feel herself tearing up. Jade was bringing back memories that she wanted to suppress. She had begged God to let her have a normal life like other little children, but her young life had been filled with strange men and drugs. Moving from place to place to stay a step ahead of Child Welfare Services kept her from making friends.

"Are you okay?" Jade asked, watching Lila wipe a tear from her cheek.

"Yeah."

"Can you sleep in here with me tonight? You can have the top bunk if you want. Then I'll pray for you so you won't be sad," Jade said as she picked up the dolls they were playing with.

"Well, let's ask your mom, okay?"

Lila pulled herself together and helped Jade put up the toys they were playing with before they headed downstairs. Crystal had called them down to have cake and ice cream. Lila could have stayed in Jade's room and played all day. She wondered what Samuel thought about her spending all her time with his niece. She certainly hadn't planned to relax so quickly, but Crystal and Jade made it easy. Jade took her hand when they were done, and they joined Crystal and Samuel at the kitchen table.

"We thought we were going to have to send the MPs up to get you guys," Samuel said, smiling.

"Jade is a very good friend." Lila was smiling too. "She asked me to bunk in her room tonight. I told her I'd have to ask her mother."

"Jade, baby, you can't keep Lila up in your room all day. Uncle Samuel wants to spend some time with her too."

"He can spend time with her when he's somewhere else," Jade said.

"Now, come on. You know you have to share," Crystal said, shaking her head at Jade. Lila loved children's honesty. They just said what they wanted to say without any reservations.

"Okay, Mommy. Uncle Samuel, is Lila going to my play with us tomorrow?"

"Yes ma'am," Samuel said, and he winked at Lila.

"Good. Then I'll share her today. But tonight she promised to stay with me if it's okay with Mommy." Samuel laughed.

"Lila, is that okay with you. Jade usually doesn't take to people so well, but she seems to really like you. We'll understand if you want some privacy in the guestroom."

"Crystal, I would be honored to have a sleepover with Jade. We have a lot in common. We both love Barbie."

"Yeahhh, thanks Mommy. Now I can pray for Lila. She was sad for a little while. She cried. I don't want her to be sad," Jade said, who now looked exaggeratedly sad for Lila.

"Is there something I can do, Lila?" Crystal asked.

"I can leave if you need to talk," Samuel said as he stood up.

Lila shook her head. "I'm fine. Jade just reminded me of my sister. I missed her for a moment, but I'll try to call her when I get home."

"You can use the phone to call her from here. I don't mind," Crystal said as she scooped ice cream into crystal bowls.

"I, uh, don't know her number. It's at home," Lila lied. She didn't even know if Lisa lived in the same place anymore. She was embarrassed to call collect when she was younger, and when she did get the money, she felt bad for the time that she had let elapse between calls.

Crystal cut pieces of chocolate cake and placed them on matching crystal saucers and passed them around. They ate, talked, and laughed like old friends. Jade told funny stories about her uncle when he visited them in Hawaii and Crystal told her how Samuel had mentioned her name before she finally met her and how happy she was that Samuel was happy. Lila felt like she was at a family reunion.

Samuel picked up the conversation when Crystal was finished talking about how much fun they had growing up in the Army. Samuel mimicked his father when he gave him the talk about joining the Army and serving his country. He had convinced his son to do four years, which was how Samuel paid for his education and the business he and three of his buddies, including her aunt's husband, Leonard, built. Lila admired Samuel for all he had accomplished. He had it going on, but his attitude was laid back. She was starting to like Samuel.

Crystal was a registered nurse at the base hospital, and they had one other sister, Carol, living in Kansas with her husband and three children. Samuel told her that their father had died three years ago and Carol had taken her mother in to live with her family. Samuel said their mother enjoyed being there to help Carol with the kids, and he said, all her friends lived in the area. She was also a few hours from Samuel, so he could help Carol if she ever needed anything.

Lila was not used to family being this close. The only one that she could truly say loved her was her Aunt Barbara. Her mother was too busy with her own life, and she did not know who her father was. She remembered meeting her grandfather briefly, but she would never forget her grandmother, who treated Lila as if she was a crack-head ready to steal her purse. She remembered her grandmother saying, "You gone end up just like yo nasty mama. I can see it in yo eyes." Lila hadn't cared what she thought. She had only just met her and didn't want to ever see her again. I fact, her grandmother died the Sunday after Lila met her, but Lila felt no remorse because she never knew her. Lila and her mother didn't even go to the funeral, which was the topic of an ongoing argument between her Aunt Barbara and her mother.

Lila was beginning to feel alive sitting in this house with these people. She had been walking around like a dead person for years, but she felt life stirring inside of her now. She thought she wanted Andrew, but he only reminded her of what she was doing wrong. Everything was good in their relationship as far as she was concerned until she was alone and had time to think about him having a wife he left for their little flings. She hadn't allowed herself to think about having someone for herself because life had taught her that she was only good for one thing.

Samuel had come along and changed all of that. He hadn't even mentioned sex, and here she was in his sister's house enjoying good conversation and a warmth she embraced and wanted to last for a long time. Her world was changing, and though she was a little scared, she looked forward to what was coming next.

CHAPTER 17

"Did Lila leave a number where she would be? I've called her cell phone, but she's not answering," Andrew said, looking at Joe as if he'd hid her in his bottom drawer and wouldn't tell him where she was.

"Lila took leave, Mister Blake. Remember?" Joe answered as he opened one of the envelopes Gladys had left on his desk. He was not Lila's keeper, but she was definitely a keeper. He smiled at his own joke and ignored Andrew. Let him go ask someone else, he thought. He was busy.

Andrew returned to his office. He hadn't meant to act as if he needed Lila, but she hadn't returned his calls and he wanted to spend some time with her before his wife got back from her "girlfriend getaway." Angie and three of her close friends always went away right after the benefit to shop for presents and get their spa treatments. He had been looking forward to Angie's absence because he thought he could have Lila for the weekend.

He called her cell phone at least six times and she still hadn't answered. He paced his office and tried to remember if she said where she was going. He was acting like an addict looking for a hit and he knew it — it made him uncomfortable. He and Angie were getting along great, and she had even consented to starting their family, but for some reason he still needed Lila. He dialed her cell again but got the same message. He slammed his cell phone down and opened the mail on his desk. If he could contact her by tonight, they would at least have one night together.

The intercom in his office came on: "Mister Blake, there is a call for you on line one," Gladys said. Andrew snatched the phone up hoping it was Lila, but it was his father saying that he and his mother had gotten home safe. Andrew mumbled something and hung up.

Gladys appeared at the door of his office. "A Mister Manigault is here to see you, Mister Blake. I think he's the guy who is donating some money for the hospital library because his mother enjoyed her last stay there or something. Gladys said flipping her curly bang out of her eye. She turned and motioned for Mister Manigault to come in and left Andrew with him. Andrew wished Gladys would find another job somewhere, but she seemed to be content to terrorize the people in their office. There was no good reason to fire Gladys other than the fact that she was slow and mean spirited. If there was a way, he would have done it by now. He hated that she was the one taking Lila's place while she was gone.

Andrew walked around the desk and shook the man's hand. They talked for an hour about the library and how much Mister Manigault's mother had enjoyed her stay there. They actually had a lot in common. Troy Manigault was from Louisiana also, and he had done very well for himself in the stock market. He was retired from the government, where he had held a very high grade, and had taken a job as the city contractor in the small town right outside of Juniper. They didn't have a hospital and his mother had to be rushed to Juniper for her bypass. His mother had told him about the excellent care she received there and wanted to show her appreciation, joining her son in donating to the library.

They talked about local politics and how they could support one another in the future. Troy said that Black Rock needed to get more involved with the communities around it. They were starting a new housing project and expanding their clinic to add an urgent care unit. They also had a new children's recreation center under construction that would give local kids the excitement of an amusement park right in their own town. Andrew had passed a couple of the signs that the new contractor had put up on I-15, and he had even thought about buying one of the new houses for his parents.

"You know what, Troy? I'm glad you stopped in. I had some plans to move my parents to Black Rock. It's a new town and pretty quiet, and you have a small retirement community started already. A couple of their friends moved over from Colorado to be near their children, and my parents visit them quite often. Tell your man to give me a call when he starts to sell. I want to take my parents over and let them pick the lot they want."

"I sure will, Andrew. I'll see you at the ribbon cutting," Troy said, putting his hand out for Andrew to shake. Andrew was glad Troy had stopped by. He had more than one plan for the property he was thinking about buying in Black Rock. He'd heard that the more secluded homes were being built with a small guest house on the property, the perfect place for his late night and weekend excursions. Thinking about the property reminded him that he still hadn't heard from Lila. He dialed her cell again.

CHAPTER 18

Lila had a good night's sleep, and then they paid a visit to the Lego Land Play Ground and later saw a movie. Crystal had prepared a sack lunch for each of them, and they sat in the concession area and ate their sandwiches and chatted with the people that were around them before going to Jade's school play.

Lila had completely forgotten to turn her cell phone on after arriving at Crystal's place. She pressed the phone on and checked her mailbox. Andrew's number popped up several times. Lila slipped out to the bathroom in the middle of the second grade's rendition of "Joy to the World." Jade's class was not scheduled to perform until after the break, so she had time. She excused herself and went outside, standing just beyond the entrance to the gymnasium where the Christmas program was being held to dial Andrew's number. He answered on the first ring.

"Andrew, is there something wrong?" Lila asked. His name was listed in her missed calls list at least ten times.

"Where are you? I've been trying to get hold of you so we can spend some time together. Angie's gone for the weekend, so if we hurry, we can spend tonight and tomorrow together." Lila thought about his offer and wanted to hang up. She had been seeing Andrew for at least three months and not once had it bothered her to be his "lady in waiting" until today.

"Uh, Andrew, I'm in San Diego. I can't leave right now. Maybe we can plan to see each other another weekend." Lila squeezed her eyes shut and waited for him to respond.

"Oh, it's like that, is it Lila? You found somebody else?"

Lila inhaled loudly before she spoke again. "Andrew, I have a life too. I don't complicate yours, so I'd appreciate it if you do the same for me."

Andrew was not prepared for her answer. Usually Lila jumped at the chance to spend time with him. After their little trip to Kansas, Lila had come back with a new thirst for him, but now she was basically asking him to get lost. Andrew felt a warning bell go off. Someone had probably got to her somehow. He knew he had not been able to see Lila very often after the Kansas trip, but he didn't want Angie to be suspicious.

"So, what are you saying, Lila? You need some space, or you just want to stop now?"

"Andrew, I'll come back on Sunday and we'll spend the whole day together, but I can't break away right now. Where should I meet you tomorrow?" Lila hoped he accepted her offer and stopped trying to pry into her business.

"I guess I can accept that. Meet me at the Days Inn in Black Rock. No need for you to come all the way into town. There will be less chance we will run into people we know."

"I'll be there about eleven or twelve o'clock. Keep the bed warm for me." Lila felt horrible after she ended the call. She realized that she was just going through the motions with Andrew. She decided that, as soon as she was back at work, she would tell him it was over.

Lila went back into the gym just in time to see Jade's class march up and get in place for their play. Jade was an elf in a play entitled "Santa's little Helpers," and she shined brighter than any of the other kids. Her smile lit up the stage when she uttered her three words: "Not Me Santa." Crystal jumped up and down when Jade finished with her speaking part while Samuel snapped pictures.

After the play, families crowded together to hug their little stars and to take pictures. Lila smiled when Jade turned to her and asked her to get in the picture. Jade made her feel like part of the family. Lila realized that she was learning a very valuable lesson from a very young teacher. She thought, maybe that's why Jesus said, "Unless you become as one of these little ones, you will not enter into the kingdom of heaven."

"Lila, you've been a little quiet. Is there something wrong?" Samuel asked after they were in the car and had their seatbelts on.

"Oh, I'm just a little tired, I guess," Lila lied. She was confused by all the new thoughts invading her mind. She had been completely satisfied with her so-called relationship with Andrew before this trip to Dan Diego. The decisions she knew she had to make were rushing at her faster than she could handle them. She sat back and watched the ships go by the small waterfront of the Doubletree Hotel. The lights were beautiful, reflecting off of the water and sparkling in the night. Lila almost asked Samuel to stop so she could walk along the water's edge and inhale the smells of seafood coming from the restaurant on the pier, but Jade was asleep and she knew they should get her home to bed.

"We probably wore her out, little brother. Lila, sleep in the guestroom tonight. Jade won't even know you aren't in the room. She'll be out until tomorrow morning."

"I have to leave tomorrow, so if you don't mind, when I wake up I want to see her little smiling face hanging over me."

"She hooked you too," Samuel said smiling. "I warned you that she was contagious." Crystal's ear to ear smile said how proud she was of her little miracle baby: Jade was a premature baby and had only weighed three pounds at birth. Crystal and her husband dubbed her "little miracle" as soon as they saw her, and she had proved to be just that in every life that touched hers, a miracle.

It only took fifteen minutes to get from the gym to Crystal's quarters again. Samuel carried Jade to her room so Crystal could get her ready for bed. Crystal asked Lila to put on a pot of the Starbuck's coffee she saved for company. Samuel came down to the kitchen and sat on one of the stools at the kitchen counter.

"Well Lila, did you enjoy your visit?" Samuel asked, picking up the glass top to the cake plate and cutting himself a slice.

"I did. Thank you for bringing me here, but now I need to get back to Juniper before ten tomorrow. Is that a problem?"

"No. You want to leave tonight or early in the morning?"

"Tomorrow, if you don't mind. When were you planning to leave?"

"I'll just leave tomorrow too. Crystal and Jade are doing great, and I've done my duty as an uncle — so it's back to work for me. When do I get my next date?"

"I didn't know we were on a date. When will you be back in town?"

"When do you want me to be?" Lila turned the coffeepot on and sat down beside Samuel.

"Oh, I just say when and you come to me?"

"It's that easy. It may require me to change some things around on my schedule, but you're worth it."

Lila turned her face away so Samuel couldn't see her expression. He didn't know what kind of person she was. "Save your charm for someone who's worth it, Samuel. I am not the person you think I am."

Samuel turned Lila's face toward him again. "Then who are you? Are you going to tell me that you weren't the sensitive young lady who played with my niece and just about cried when she said her little speech on that stage? I think I know who you are, Lila."

"You only see what I am when I am here. I have a life in Juniper, and I'm not so proud of some parts of that life. I wish I could magically change some of the things I've done, but I know that's impossible."

"Then start today with what you can change, my lady. Tomorrow is another day. How about dealing with today? Believe me, I've done some things I wish I could erase too, but I just had to learn how to deal with my mistakes."

"Samuel, when I said I wasn't seeing anyone on a regular basis, I lied. I'm seeing someone, but he's not really who I want. I was just lonely at the time and started something that I really don't want now." Lila couldn't believe she was going to tell Samuel about Andrew, but she felt he needed to know.

"Is that why you need to get back tomorrow?" Samuel asked.

"Um, hm. He's been calling me since I left Juniper, but I was having so much fun I forgot to turn on my cell phone."

"So what are you going to do?"

"I don't know. I just don't know." Lila turned away from Samuel. It was hard to explain to him, but she felt relieved talking about her situation.

"Again, I don't want to complicate your life, but I think you should slow down and find out what you really want." Samuel got up and walked around to face Lila. "We're still friends, no matter what." As hard as it was to say, he had to say it. He didn't want her with him if she was emotionally tied to someone else.

"It's a little late. You already complicated everything. I know you didn't mean to, but you did."

Lila and Samuel talked for a few more minutes before going up to bed. The same questions still hung in the air. Would she walk away from Andrew and try to make it with Samuel? Lila was in deep thought when she entered the Barbie shrine. She blinked back tears as she prepared for her shower. Life was so easy just yesterday.

CHAPTER 19

Lila checked into the hotel in Black Rock and ordered lunch for herself while she waited for Andrew. Samuel had been quite nice to her when he dropped her at the hotel, and he told her she could call him whenever she needed him. She changed into one of the sheer outfits that Andrew had given her and slipped on her housecoat before room service delivered her meal. She thought about Samuel again and decided to call him. She looked through her purse for her cell phone and dialed his number. Samuel picked up on the third ring.

"Are you at home yet?" Lila asked.

"Uh, no. I just dropped you off about an hour ago. Planes are fast, but you have to get on them first. I'm at the rental car agency turning in the car. What's up?"

"I just wanted to hear your voice, I guess. What time do you leave?" Lila asked, trying to keep him on the phone.

"My plane leaves at two-thirty. Are you coming to watch my plane take off?" Samuel laughed.

"Okay, Mister Joke Man. See if I ask about you again."

"Ahhh, don't get mad, Lila. I'm just messing with you. Like I said, I'm turning in the rental, and I'm next in line. I'll call you when I get home."

"Okay. See you in the funny papers." Lila remembered her aunt saying that to her when she went off to school each morning.

"Okay, beautiful. Talk to you later." Samuel clicked the phone off and smiled. At least she was thinking about him. That was a start.

Lila opened the door for room service. They had been knocking for a minute before she noticed. She didn't realize she was smiling when she answered the door. The waiter, a young Hispanic with a big smile, stood before her with a tray on a cart. He did a head-to-toe inspection and then lumbered in with the tray. He asked if she wanted him to set up the table, but she declined. She knew Andrew should be coming shortly and didn't want the waiter to see him. She gave him a tip and danced over to the table and sat down to eat. She was feeling good. Maybe Angie would come home early and Andrew would have to cancel on her. The room was already paid for, and if she wanted to, she could get a massage and a facial and go home.

Andrew had seen the room service attendant enter Lila's room, and he waited until the man left, then made sure the coast was clear before he got out of the rental car. He raced up the few steps and tapped on the door. Lila peeked out before she opened the door. She took a deep breath and stepped aside for Andrew to enter.

"Hi, beautiful. I like the outfit. Someone has good taste," Andrew said as he walked slowly around Lila. Lila stepped back without thinking. She felt naked in front of Andrew and wanted to run from the room and change. Everything she thought she wanted from him seemed to make her feel dirty now.

"What's the matter with you? You're jumping like I'm gonna hurt you. You know better than that." Andrew pulled Lila down on the bed with him and kissed her neck.

"I'm just not feeling well today. I was going to call you and cancel, but you seemed so excited about tonight, I just came anyway," Lila lied, holding her stomach.

"I'm glad you made it. Can't you take a pill? I want to make love to you all night," Andrew said, stripping off his shirt and pants. Lila stared at him in amazement. She realized for the first time since they had been seeing each other that Andrew only wanted to be pleased. In the beginning, he had lavished gifts on her, but slowly the gifts stopped coming and the demand on her time started to increase.

"I'll take something and then maybe we can do something later." Lila got up, picked up her purse, and pretended to look for something. She rarely had headaches and so she didn't even have an aspirin in her purse. She slipped a mint out of the case and popped it in her mouth, then sipped some water from the glass the waiter had left. She went back to the bed and slid under the covers. She thought Andrew would do the same, but he came over to her side and rubbed her stomach.

"You think you may be pregnant?" Andrew asked like an expectant child. She knew he wanted a baby more than anything, but Lila wasn't sure she wanted to commit to that. She had told him in the beginning that she would gladly have his baby, but after she gave it some serious thought, she couldn't see bringing a baby into the world for a married man. The child would be the one to suffer, and Lord knows she had suffered enough to know she couldn't put a child through that. Right now she would say anything to keep him away from her.

"I am late." It wasn't a complete lie. Her cycle was definitely erratic. Andrew smiled from ear to ear. He jumped over her and slid under the covers.

"That's all you had to say. You get your rest. That might be my legacy lying in your belly." Lila kept her face towards the wall. She didn't want to see Andrew's face.

CHAPTER 20

Lila bustled through the office with letters and packages prepared for mailing. She had come back to work with a new attitude. Andrew had given her time to herself because he thought she was pregnant, not even touching her that night in the hotel in Black Rock, and she had talked to Samuel for at least an hour after she returned home. She felt like a new person after talking to Samuel. He made her laugh and always had something positive to say. She had to find a way to tell Andrew she didn't want to see him anymore, and soon.

"What kind of stuff you smoking, girl? You've been running around here like a crack-head. Give me some of them pills. I need some energy too," Gladys said, rolling the mail cart around the office collecting outgoing mail.

"I am not on drugs, Gladys. I'm just happy. You remember what that is, don't you?"

"How you know if I'm happy or not?"

Lila started to keep her mouth shut, but Gladys had pushed a button and she felt like talking. "You don't act happy, Gladys. The only time you seem happy is when someone else is miserable. Now I don't mean any harm, but you are always mumbling and grumbling. Look around you, Gladys. You have something a lot of people wish they had."

"And what's that?" Gladys said with her arms folded tightly across her chest.

"A job, a man, a home, some clothes, and food on your table," Lila said, waving her hands in the air like a television evangelist pumping up the congregation.

"You found Jesus, didn't you?" Gladys asked, slowly walking toward Lila. Gladys remembered when her cousin had found religion and had started talking to any family member who would listen about her great discovery.

"No. I just know that all of us here are fortunate. But enough of that, Gladys, I don't want to stop you from working, but nothing is going to bring me down today." Lila dumped her load of mail in the cart and headed back to her chair.

"There's a call on line one for Lila," Joe hollered over the commotion Gladys and Lila were making.

"Got it," Lila said, and she picked up the extension on Gladys' desk. Gladys gave her the evil eye but otherwise ignored her.

"This is Lila. Speak now or forever hold your peace," Lila said into the receiver.

"Lila, is that you? Please say I've got the right number," a familiar woman's voice said.

"Lisa!" Lila shouted.

"Yes. Oh God, I'm so glad I found you. I thought you were dead." Lisa began to sob uncontrollably. Lila couldn't believe her sister was on the other end of the phone.

"I'm not dead, Lisa. Don't cry. I'm okay. You know we were on the move so much and I didn't have the address anymore."

"Well we have each other now. Guess what?"

"What?"

"I'm getting married in January. Can you believe it? One of the ragamuffins is finally going to have a real family." Lila and Lisa had been called ragamuffins by the people who watched them move from apartment to apartment in the neighborhood and then move back to their grandmother's house. Lisa's father finally got tired and took her to live with him.

"Congratulations, Lisa. I hope he makes you happy."

"Yes, I'm happy, and I want you here with me through the whole process. I'll pay for your ticket to New York, Lila. I just want you here with me. Can you take two weeks off in January?" Lisa asked excitedly.

"Well I..."

"Oh Lila, don't worry about my father. He lives in another city, and he's only coming down for the weekend of my wedding. Please say you'll come. I miss you so much. We've got a lot of catching up to do, like you working in the mayor's office. I'm so proud of you, La-La." Lila hadn't heard her nickname in years. She couldn't speak for a moment. She was in an office full of her coworkers and she didn't want to break down, but her eyes welled up with tears.

"Are you there, La-La? Don't worry about anybody standing in our way now. You are still my baby sister no matter how old you are."

Lila rushed into the open mailroom door and closed it behind her. She let out the cry she had been stifling. She tried telling Lisa that she would be there, but she was crying so hard her voice was muffled. Her prayers were being answered. "I guess that means you're coming," Lisa said, and Lila heard her blow her nose.

"Yes. I miss you too, Lisa. We made it, didn't we?" Lila said, wiping her face with the sleeve of her shirt.

"We did. I wish I could see old Mrs. Randall. Remember, she used to come out of her apartment and point at us and tell her kids to stay away from us?" Lila had forgotten all about that. Mrs. Randall was mean and so were her kids.

"Oh, I remember. I saw her older boy when I graduated from high school. He was dating one of the freshman girls. You know that fool was at least twenty-five," Lila said, now remembering the elder Randall boy's face when he recognized who she was. He had sauntered over and tried to say something to her, but she pushed past him and hurried inside the school.

"I wouldn't put it past him. All them kids were bad. Our mother should have told us to stay away from them."

"It's so good to hear your voice, Lisa. Give me your number so I can call you when I get home. This lady that I work with will be hollering about getting in here in a minute, and I'm not in the mood for her grumpy behind right now." Lisa gave Lila her number right before Gladys started pounding on the mailroom door.

"Lila. Open this door! Some people have work to do!" Gladys shouted, pounding on the door. Lila opened the door and walked by Gladys and smiled. No one could mess up her mood now. She was on top of the world. She was going to see her sister get married and catch up with her on all the things they had missed in each other's lives. She couldn't wait to call Samuel and tell him. Lila smiled when she thought about calling Samuel. She wanted to share everything with Samuel.

She rushed home after work to call Lisa. They talked about old times and briefly talked about their mother. Lisa said that she heard through the grapevine that their mother was living in a welfare hotel. She didn't have the address, so she couldn't invite her, not that she wanted to anyway. Lisa was getting married the last week in January and had been excited when Lila said she'd like to have a guest come to the wedding with her.

Lila now knew for certain that she wanted a fresh start. Andrew couldn't be a part of her new life. He belonged to someone else. She sat down and wrote the letter she had been putting off for at least a month.

CHAPTER 21

Angie brushed her hair out of the wrap she had slept in and flipped it with her hands. Her hairdresser had outdone herself this year. Her hair looked healthy and bounced every time she moved. Everything in her life seemed to be going the way she wanted it. Andrew had started to perform as if he had taken some classes, and now, after years of loathing the idea, she really wanted to have a baby. She had stopped taking her birth control but hadn't told Andrew yet. She wanted to surprise him when she conceived. Josh was on vacation in Canada with his parents. She had a story ready for him when he got back. The affair was over, and she didn't want to waste any time with good-byes.

Angie slid on her red gabardine pants and matching sweater. She applied a little lip gloss and shook her hair out again. Andrew was taking her to a play after his meeting in Los Angeles on Monday. They were now on their way to her parent's home to have Sunday dinner. Angie could recite what would happen from the beginning to the end of their dinner.

Her mother would go on and on about how fortunate she was to have Andrew and tell her father and sisters how her friends compliment her at church because her daughter married well. Then she'd prance around the kitchen and ask Andrew what his favorite things were even though she knew quite well and made them every time they came to dinner. Andrew would then turn to her and ask her if she was taking notes. There was no way she was cooking up any collards, fried chicken, roast and seasoned potatoes with cornbread. He was lucky she put things in the crock pot on the days she let Gayle, their housekeeper and cook, off for one night.

Angie laughed when she thought about her father's comments. He had always liked Andrew, and as soon as her mother started her little spiel, her father would say, "Look how far blacks have come Anna. We got us a part of history right under our roof." Her sisters, Audrey and Alyssa, would look at their parents as if they were speaking Spanish and roll their eyes. They didn't care about Andrew's position, and both thought him a "straight country bama."

"Teenagers don't understand how important it is for us to move into those kinds of positions," her mother would say to her and stare at the teenagers. Audrey was fifteen and Melissa was sixteen, and they had one thing on their mind — boys.

PostPartum

Angie broke out of her reverie and called to Andrew to help her with the boxes of clothes she was giving to her mother for a rummage sale they were having at her church, in spite of the fact that church was another sore spot between Angie and her mother. She was tired of her mother going on and on about which nice young people of their mutual acquaintance go to church and how they are so blessed and prosperous, blah, blah, blah. None of them were living in the mayor's mansion, going to prestigious places, and meeting exciting and sometimes famous people. If anybody was blessed and prosperous it was her.

Angie and Andrew arrived at her childhood home in time to witness an ambulance racing out of her parents' driveway. Her heart began to race when Andrew pressed on the brake and pulled out of the way so the ambulance could pass. She could hear screaming coming from the house when she jumped out of the car and raced up the lawn. Audrey and Melissa were rocking in an embrace on the floor when she entered the house and her Aunt Brenda was on her knees comforting her nieces.

"What's going on?" Angie heard herself screech. "Where are Daddy and Mother?" Andrew was at her side instantly, feeling the panic in the house and waiting for a response from her aunt. Her Aunt Brenda refused to meet their eyes when she spoke.

"Your father had a heart attack, Angie. Your mom was cooking in the kitchen when I heard her scream. I came into the kitchen to see what was wrong, and he was lying on the floor." Angie felt her body go limp. She could see that her aunt was still moving her mouth but she couldn't hear her. Someone had made a mistake. Her father was only sixty-eight, and he was healthy. The last time they talked, he was going on and on about how good he felt and how he couldn't wait to see them at dinner. Andrew was leading her to the couch, but she needed the bathroom. She felt like throwing up.

"Sit down, baby. You gotta focus. We need to get to the hospital so we can let your father know that we're there for him. Angie bobbed her head up and down and sat down. She needed to gather her strength so she could go to the hospital and comfort her father, but her aunt was shaking her head and silently crying while she cradled her sisters.

"Why are you shaking your head, Aunt Brenda? I need to be with my father. Do you hear me! You don't run this house!" Her aunt was always trying to boss them around, telling her mother they were too smart-mouthed and fast. She was grown now and didn't have to take her mess.

"It's too late, Angie. They couldn't revive him." Her aunt and sisters began to wail louder.

"You better stop your lying, Aunt Brenda." Angie jumped up and ran frantically through the house looking for her mother, but then she remembered the ambulance. Someone had to ride with her father, and that someone would be her mother. But when Angie started up the stairs for the bathroom, she saw her mother standing on the landing. She felt like she was moving in slow motion up the stairs. Her mother's eyes were red from crying. Angie shook her head and begged her mother to tell her that her aunt was wrong. Her mother opened her arms for her, and then everything went black.

CHAPTER 22

Lila slipped the note into Andrew's briefcase while putting some other papers on his desk. She almost passed out when Joe sauntered in and dropped off a tape of the banquet they had attended on Thanksgiving. Then she realized he probably would not suspect anything because she was always in an out of Andrew's office. Her voice had just sounded a little higher pitched than normal when she greeted him, but Joe didn't seem to notice.

Lila made sure she left the briefcase open in case Joe came back into the office again, not that it mattered. She knew that she was just being paranoid. He wouldn't have cared, but it made her feel better. Andrew was very busy helping his wife with her father's funeral and would only come in for a few hours today. They had heard through the grapevine that Angie had passed out and was rushed to the hospital.

Lila sat down at her desk and breathed a sigh of relief until Mrs. Blake walked up to her desk. She had just relaxed when Angie appeared in front of her.

"Excuse me, but do you know where Andrew is right now?" Angie asked Lila. Lila could tell that Angie had been crying. She still had on her sunglasses inside the building and her voice was quivering.

"I, uh, think he may be in the conference room. Would you like to sit in the lounge? I could get you something to drink and stick my head in the conference room and let him know you're here."

"I'll take the drink, but I'd rather wait in his office. Thank you." Lila nodded and asked what kind of drink she wanted. She hoped Angie wouldn't notice the envelope lying in Andrew's briefcase. Lila got the Coke Angie asked for and hurried back to the conference room. She opened the door wide enough to get Andrew's attention, and he waved her over.

"Your wife is in your office. Will you be much longer?" Andrew told Lila to inform Angie he would be with her in fifteen minutes.

"Mrs. Blake, Mister Blake said he can see you in fifteen minutes. They're wrapping up the meeting right now." Lila handed her the Coke and glass of ice. "I'm really sorry about your father passing," Lila said sincerely.

Angie nodded, smiled, and turned toward the window. She was still in shock and didn't want to talk about her father's death, especially with someone she did not know very well. Angie waited until Lila left the office before she got up and stood before the window.

Everything looked bleak and dull to her. It was dark outside, and it had been drizzling all day, which added to her mood. She circled Andrew's desk and moved a couple of things around in his briefcase when she saw the edge of a little note card sticking out of one of the pockets. Normally, she wouldn't bother any of his things, but she was curious. The envelope did not look like official correspondence and had a definite feminine quality to it. It was not sealed, so she opened it.

CHAPTER 23

Dennis Damon Johnson was laid to rest on the second Saturday in December. Angie sat slouched beside her mother and sisters, high on the pills prescribed by the emergency room doctor who attended to her the night her father died. Andrew sat with the pallbearers as the minister from the Johnson's church was preaching. Andrew had suggested that Angie be taken home and not attend the gravesite ceremony and her mother had agreed. She was in no condition to watch the casket being lowered into the ground. He couldn't put his finger on it, but something else was bothering Angie. She had been very quiet and subdued lately.

When the minister was finished, one of the ladies from the choir sang "Precious Lord," which sent the crowd into a moaning and wailing frenzy. After the solo, a friend of the family gave Mister Johnson's eulogy, and the pastor prayed and dismissed the crowd. One hour was all that was needed to put a period at the end of a life. Andrew thought about all that had transpired in the last week, and he decided it was time for him to get his life together. He wanted to work on his marriage, but he wanted Lila too. Angie needed him now, and he had vowed to be there for better or for worse. His life was more complicated than he wanted it to be, and yet, he could not seem to give up any of the complications.

Two usher's helped Angie and Janice, her father's sister, into the limousine that would take them back to the house. Neither could attend the grave-side vigil. Angie was too distraught, and Janice had a heart condition and was advised by her doctor not to push herself. Andrew had tried to make eye contact with Angie, but she kept her head down until she disappeared into the limousine.

Andrew felt a tugging at his heart when the casket entered the ground. He would miss his father-in-law's joking and the kind words he'd been famous for at their Sunday meal. He thought about his own father and made a mental note to call his parents as soon as the ceremony was over. His parents were out of the country and could not make it to the funeral, but they had sent their condolences and a beautiful floral arrangement.

CHAPTER 24

Angie ran her fingers across the obituary that she was handed at her father's funeral. The holiday season would now be forever darkened by the passing of her father two weeks before Christmas. Not only had she lost her father, but she had found a note in her husband's briefcase that confirmed her suspicions of infidelity. She knew she had no right to be upset because she had been just as guilty as Andrew, but somehow, the pain was not lessened by this realization. A few minutes passed before she set the paper down and stared out of her bedroom window. It was December, but the sun was shining and it was seventy degrees. "How can the sun shine when my father is dead?" she thought as the tears began to fall again.

She had been the first born and an only child for the first eighteen years of her life. In short, she was spoiled rotten, and her mother had often told her father only half-jokingly that they would never be able to find anyone to take her off their hands. Angie had surprised them and had started working at a local mall while she was still in high school, and she had even finished two years of college. Her father bought her a new car when she finished her Associates Degree, and he was the proudest father in town when she landed Andrew. He had cheered her on through good times and bad, and now he was gone.

Her Aunt Janice was asleep on their bed. She was just as devastated as Angie was. Her grandparents had taken it better than Janice had. Dennis was her little brother, even though he had grown children of his own. She kept saying, "I should have went before Dennis." She covered her aunt with the comforter that was lying on the foot of the bed and kissed her forehead. Things were changing drastically now. Angie wasn't sure where life was taking her, but she needed to start making some changes. She didn't want to end up alone and living in her mother's house again, which she had seen happen to some of her friends.

Andrew could even come home and ask her for a divorce, and she wouldn't blame him. The thought made her cry again. He'd tried so hard, but she was so "stuck on being stupid" that she couldn't see him for who he was. He finally got tired and found someone to ease the pain, the pain she had caused.

Angie wondered if the ceremony was over. There was no way she could have watched the casket being lowered into the ground, and she was glad her aunt felt the same way. She didn't want to be alone. Her mother was in shock but couldn't break away because of her loyalty to her husband. Victoria Alleen Johnson would be there for every part of the ceremony, just as her husband had been there for her for forty years. He didn't run away in the bad times, and she would not dishonor him by not attending every second of the funeral no matter how bad she felt.

The example of the perfect marriage was before her all her life, and she had been too self-absorbed to see it. Her parents' marriage was not without problems or trials, but theirs was a marriage between two people who respected one another and had each other's back. She remembered a few arguments here and there, but nothing like what she and Andrew had been doing for the last five years.

Her wants and desires had always taken precedent over anything and everything in their world. She had even isolated herself from some of her good friends, trying to be above everybody. Only two of her friends from high school showed up at the funeral, and even they hadn't tried to call her before the service to offer their condolences. Angie felt like she was alone in the world. She had even told Josh to get lost, and she knew how much he loved her. The phone rang before she could finish her thoughts.

"Hello," Angie whispered into the phone.

"Are you okay, girl? I know it's been a long time, but I know you and your daddy was tight, so I thought I better call and check on you."

"Jaynelle. Is that you?" Angie asked, praying she was right.

"Who else you know bold enough to call your bousie behind after you ditched a sister," Jaynelle said, obviously trying to cheer Angie up.

"Who you calling bousie? You still pimpin'," Angie said, laughing. Jaynelle had at least five brothers when they were in school, and they were doing all kinds of business for her, so her friends had started teasing her by calling her a pimp. She favored Laila Ali in her looks, and she was built like her to. Jaynelle didn't take no mess, and she could whip any of the brothers in their school.

"Now why you gotta bring up the past? You know I gave up pimpin' when I started working at the childcare center."

"I cannot believe Jaynelle Henderson is working at a childcare center. Why you wanna scare the babies like that?" Angie said, laughing again.

"For your information, the kids love me, but they better be scared cause I ain't playing. I need their little lunch money on time every day." Jaynelle laughed, but there was an awkward pause before Jaynelle began speaking again.

"I know you hurting, Angie. It's hard losing someone that close, but I just wanted you to know that, even though you moved on up, some of us down here still care about you."

"Jaynelle, you guys were always welcome in my house. Didn't you know that?"

"It's hard to know that when you don't return calls and then don't show up to our class reunion. I know you're busy with your little clubs and charities, but you shouldn't forget about your friends."

"Dang, Jaynelle. I couldn't see that. I thought I had to do all this stuff so I wouldn't look like one of those wives who didn't know her place. I just got caught up in all this social stuff, but losing Daddy made me wake up quick. I didn't even have anyone close I could talk to since Andrew entered politics."

"Well, I'll be over there with Mama's famous potato salad and some strawberries and cream. You know how we do it. I hope you got some rum. It's daiquiri time!" Jaynelle hollered. Angie almost started to cry again when she thought about their daiquiri nights when one of them was hurt or had some man trouble in college. She could hear someone in the background talking while Jaynelle was talking.

"Who you talking to, Jay?" She felt comfortable enough to call her friend by her nickname now. She would not make the mistake of not talking with her again.

"This country behind bama called Tanya came in here with a can of pork and beans, saying, 'You got some onions cause I gotta take some baked beans over to Angie's.' Who takes baked beans to a funeral, girl? I hate her. I told you we should have let her mama take her back to South Carolina when we was in tenth grade. She crazy!" They all busted out laughing.

"You let Tanya bring her beans and you bring the potato salad. Come over now before the mourners get here. I want to hug you two before I get smothered by the rest of the town. Hurry up. I can taste those daiquiris already." Angie hung up the phone and ran into the bathroom to wash her face and put on a pair of jeans and her college t-shirt.

"I'm still learning, Daddy. Thanks for the lesson." Angie blew a kiss up to heaven where she knew her father was watching her, checked on her Aunt Janice, and then rushed down the stairs to welcome her friends.

CHAPTER 25

Lila paced the floor wondering whether or not Andrew was going to call. She had already rehearsed what she was going to say. Samuel had been calling and writing her ever since he went back to Kansas, and she knew that he was the man she wanted in her life. He made her feel important and needed. She had even started looking for another job so she wouldn't be tempted to see Andrew again. The college had called her for an interview, and she was spending Saturday morning at the mall looking for an outfit to wear to the interview.

Samuel had invited her to Kansas for Christmas and she had accepted. She thought he was going to ask her to stay at his place, but he asked if she wanted him to get her a hotel room or stay at her aunt's place. She decided to stay with her aunt again. They never got to have breakfast alone, and she was looking forward to cooking in her aunt's big kitchen. She thought about what Andrew said when she asked him why he wasn't trying to get her into bed. He simply replied, "I'm trying to get you into my heart."

All men want sex, at least all the men she had run into, and so she had to believe he had some motive she could not discern. She had to get to the bottom of what Andrew was trying to say to her.

"So, you're saying that you *do* want to have sex with me then," Lila asked.

"No, you were the one talking about sex. I want to make love to you, but everything has to be right, Lila."

"Are you making excuses 'cause there's something wrong with you physically or you don't really want to? I'll understand if something's wrong. I'll stay with you no matter what."

"There is nothing wrong with me Lila, and I do want to make love to you. I just won't jump into bed with someone to fulfill my lust. I want more than that in a relationship, and I want a relationship with you."

"Okay. Well I'm going to take a cold shower and call you in the morning." They had ended their conversation on sex and she hadn't called him back yet. How could he not want to have sex until "everything is right," whatever that meant? He wasn't a minister, and he claimed there was nothing wrong with him physically. Lila thought she knew what men wanted, but Samuel had changed the script and now she didn't know what to do. She hadn't met one man who wanted anything but sex first and the rest somewhere down the list. They'd all wanted sex first and foremost, and they didn't even ask sometimes, but Samuel was different. She thought offering herself was the right thing to do, but maybe not. But then again, maybe when she got to Kansas, he would change his mind. She searched through her closet to find something for the interview, forgetting her shopping plans. She would worry about Samuel later.

CHAPTER 26

Andrew was glad the funeral, the burial, and anything else to do with his father-in-law's death was over. He'd been on an emotional rollercoaster ride with Angie. One minute she wanted to snuggle, and the next minute she was crying her eyes out. He'd had all he could take and finally suggested that Angie get some counseling. He even agreed to go with her, but he told her that the crying had to stop. Christmas was like a wake instead of a holiday. He'd escaped to his office several times to get away from all the mourning. He knew it would be hard for Angie's family during Christmas, but he hadn't expected them to weep and wail as if they were at the funeral all over again every day.

He'd made several calls to Lila, but she was suddenly unavailable. He'd even heard that she was looking for another job. How could she just walk away at a time like this? She had to know that he needed her after all that he'd been through.

"Andrew!" Angie shouted from the bathroom. She wondered if he was going deaf. She'd called to him three times.

"Sorry, I was trying to make a phone call. You need something?" Andrew asked, clearing the phone number from his cell phone.

"Could you get me a towel out of the closet? I don't want to get water all over the floor."

Andrew pulled a towel from the closet and took it to Angie. He was about to turn and go back into the bedroom when he noticed that her stomach was a little swollen, or maybe it was wishful thinking, he decided. He wasn't sure about her cycle any more. They'd spent too much time apart for him to know if she missed her period.

"Take a picture. It'll last longer. Why you staring at me like you crazy? You like what you see?"

"Was I staring? That's just 'cause you're so fine, girl." Andrew smiled.

"Don't even try it. You got something else on your mind, but I'll let it go for now. I'm tired. I must be getting old. I can't even work out like I used to. You sure you didn't put no roots on me."

"That's your backwards family history. My people are from the east. We don't eat the whole chicken but its feet and then hang those feet up to be read."

"Very funny, Andrew. If I wasn't so tired, I'd come cold-cock you in the back of the head."

"See what I'm saying. I rest my case."

"Ask Gayle if I can have my food in bed, and please tell her not to fry me anything. I just want a little tuna salad and some seven-up. You can bring your food up here and have dinner with me. How does that sound?"

"Sounds like a plan, but I need to go to the office for an hour. Can we have dinner at six today?" He felt funny asking about dinner. They had not shared a meal together in months. Things seemed to be changing for the better between them, but he couldn't get Lila off his mind. He just needed a little time alone, time to find her and ask if she still wanted him. He knew he was wrong to continue to want this young woman when Angie seemed to be coming around finally, but he couldn't help himself. He wanted to be the one to say their relationship was over.

"Six it is. Just tell Gayle on your way out. I'm going to take a nap." Angie dried herself off and slipped on her silk Victoria's nightshirt. Her eyes were closed before her head hit the pillow. She wasn't sure if she was exhausted because of her father's death or because she was up all hours of the night catching up with her friends.

CHAPTER 27

Lila closed her cell phone and dropped it back in her purse. Samuel had taken her to the movies on a real date and had invited her to see his house. She had let him know that she had broken it off with Andrew. Her phone began to vibrate on the way out of the movie theater.

"Samuel, I'm gonna run into the ladies room real quick before we head out."

"You want something to take back to the house with us?" Samuel asked.

"No. I'm straight. Just wait for me on the bench. It'll just take a minute."

Lila raced to the restroom so she could call Andrew and ask him to leave her alone. She had written him the letter and had even landed another job. It was time for him to stop bothering her. She'd had enough. She dialed his cell and waited for him to answer. She slipped inside a stall and prayed he would answer. He did after three rings.

"Lila. It's about time you called. Didn't you get any of my messages?" Andrew asked.

"The question is: Can't you read? I left you a note and told you that I couldn't see you anymore. I want a life with someone who is able to see me in the daytime and take me places that don't require removing your clothes. Did you not understand the note?" Lila asked angrily.

"What are you talking about? What note?" Andrew asked, confused.

"The note I slipped in your briefcase two weeks ago. Didn't you read it?" Lila stopped to think for a second. Andrew was a lot of things, but he had never lied to her. He must not have gotten the note. "Oh God," Lila cried.

"How could you be so stupid? You don't write notes like you're still in high school. You either hand me a note or you tell me face to face. My wife probably got the note." Andrew thought about that scenario for a minute and figured that was why Angie was acting so peculiar the last couple of weeks. He wondered if she had a plan to divorce him and use the note as evidence.

"All the more reason to stop calling me — I'm too stupid for a man like you. Leave me alone, Andrew. I've moved on." Lila clicked the phone off and went to find Samuel. She was truly sorry if Andrew's wife intercepted the note, but she was glad Andrew finally knew that they were over.

"Is everything okay?" Samuel asked.

"No, but it will be. I'll tell you all about it on the way to your house."

Samuel told her to wait inside the mall until he got the car. It had started snowing and she didn't have boots or a long coat. She smiled and ran to the car when he pulled to the curb, almost falling just as she reached the car door. Now she could begin her new life without any old business to hold her back. She was even thinking about moving to Kansas.

"I'm free," Lila shouted, plopping down in the passenger's seat and rubbing her hands together. It was cold, but she felt like the world had been handed to her on a platter.

"So you've told him everything and now we can move on?" Samuel asked. He had waited at least three months to finally have Lila to himself.

"Yes, and guess what? I didn't even wait for him to respond. I just said it's time to move on and hung up." Samuel laughed and winked at Lila. The world seemed like a different place after telling Andrew to go away. Dreams were forming in her head about the future. She couldn't believe that she was actually dreaming. Lila couldn't wait to tell her sister about her change. Maybe soon *she* would be planning a wedding and inviting Lisa.

Samuel's house was just as beautiful as her aunt's place, but the colors were soft browns and reds. The house felt comfortable and warm. He lit the fireplace and they took off their coats and shoes and sat together in front of the fire.

"Okay, so tell me what you expect from me?" Samuel said.

"What?"

"Don't you have some expectations for the man you want to be with?"

"Um, well, I'd like him to be honest and share things with me. I want a real relationship and all that comes with it. I'm tired of what I was doing before." Lila took Samuel's hand and squeezed it. Samuel turned to face Lila.

"I want you, and I promise I'll treat you like the queen you are. I do not believe in sex before marriage, and so I'm afraid you're going to have to consider marriage. Can you handle that?"

"Are you a Christian?"

"Yes, and proud of it."

"I thought all Christians were supposed to stay with their own kind, as in marry only other Christians."

"We're not aliens or another species, Lila, but you are right. We should not be unevenly yoked, but I had a vision about you and I'm trusting God on this."

"God is not about to waste his time on me. You may want to reconsider your vision."

CHAPTER 28

Andrew slammed his cell phone in his bag and paced the office floor. There was no other explanation for his wife's behavior and for what he had just heard from Lila about her little note going missing. Angie had gotten the note and hadn't said anything to him about it, but then again, maybe Lila forgot to put it in his briefcase and had misplaced it. He really hoped it wasn't the former case — he didn't want his wife to find out about his infidelities. He couldn't afford a scandal in his career right now. The public would surely crucify him, and Angie, the grieving wife, would look like a saint, especially after losing her father just before Christmas.

Andrew snatched up the phone and started to call Lila back to find out if she could have possibly made a mistake, but he changed his mind and cleared the phone and turned it off. This was a wakeup call for him. "No more chasing Lila around like a whipped pup," he said out loud.

The fact was, he realized, he needed Lila to boost his ego; but Angie was his wife and he still loved her. He had been trying to get back at Angie for all the pain she had caused him when she flaunted her beautiful self around town. She acted as if she didn't need him, and he had felt lonely and betrayed; but when he stopped to think about their marriage, he could understand how Angie might have felt lonely and unloved. He spent a lot of time running from one meeting to the next some times without even stopping at home for dinner. He had accepted her rejection without hesitation because his goals had blinded him to what was really happening in their home.

It was getting close to six o'clock, and so he packed up his bag and headed for home. He was looking forward to having dinner snuggled up in his bedroom with his wife. She'd been different with him lately. Maybe things were about to take a turn for the better.

CHAPTER 29

Lila stared at the ceiling and remembered what Samuel had told her about his religious convictions. He didn't seem as stuffy and fake as most of the Christians she had come across, but she couldn't imagine herself going to church every Sunday let alone liking it. Samuel was a good man and all, but their conversation had given her a lot to think about. She had asked him to take her back to her aunt's place so she could rest. She was feeling tired and a little queasy. Maybe it was all that food she ate and then filling up on popcorn at the movies.

"How did it go tonight, Lila?" her aunt asked as she wiped the cabinets down with pine-scented cleaner. The smell brought back memories of helping her aunt clean every Saturday before they went shopping, or sometimes they would just stay home and do each others hair.

"He's a Christian, Auntie. I am the last person God would want hooked up with one of his finest. Samuel said he had a vision about me and that God thinks it's okay for him to be with me. Can you believe that?

"You are a good girl, Lila. You can't let your past define your future, baby. Leave that stuff behind and race toward your new future. Samuel cares for you Lila, and although you've had some really bad times, this may be God's way of giving you a new beginning. Now, I'm not no churchy woman, but I hear that God will give you back what you missed or something like that. You deserve the best. I want to see you happy, Lila. That is my heart's desire." She stopped cleaning and leaned over to kiss the top of Lila's head like she used to when something upset her or when she was home from school sick.

"I want Samuel, but I don't know about going to church all the time."

"Don't think like that. Just take your time, and above all else, enjoy your time with him. Go to church with him and see if you like it. If you don't, you stop going and tell him what you truly feel. Samuel will respect that. Now let's talk about my niece getting married. Lisa told me you gave her my number. I was really glad to hear from her. You know I wanted to keep both of you so you could grow up together, but your mother wouldn't let me have either of you, and when Lisa's father came to get her, I understood where he was coming from. I was just sad that you two didn't get to be together."

"Auntie, I know I told you I didn't want to know who my father is, but I've changed my mind. Do you know?" Lila asked, now lying back on the couch.

"Your mother was seeing somebody who traveled for a living, but I never got to meet him. He was only around for about three months. I don't think he knew about you. At least, that's what your mother said."

"Did you ever hear his name?"

"No I didn't. I'm sorry, Lila. Betty was very secretive. I wish I could tell you more, but that's all I know. He had to be local though. Once, Betty told me she called him to take her to the grocery store. No one would come from more than an hour away to do that."

"Thank you for always being there for me, Auntie. You made a real difference in my life. I think I would be dead now, or perhaps crazy, if it wasn't for you."

"Don't talk like that, Lila. Let's talk about something exciting, like shopping for our dresses for Lisa's wedding. We need to hit the malls!" Barbara didn't like to think about what would have happened to her niece if she hadn't intervened in her life. She thanked God every day that she hadn't stopped looking for Lila. Barbara also knew that the kind of life Lila was exposed to had left some scars. She begged Lila to go to counseling, but the young girl was too ashamed of what had happened to her to tell anyone, and Barbara didn't want to press her. She still tried to interject the counseling idea into her niece's head but was met with a firm no. Maybe Samuel was the one to bring the healing she knew Lila needed.

CHAPTER 30

Lila hurried to the waiting room at Jet Lines to meet her aunt. They had made their flight arrangements so Lisa would only have to come to the airport one time. Lila had begged her sister to let them take a taxi so she could spend her time relaxing, but Lisa insisted on coming to the airport.

Lila found the waiting area where her aunt said she would meet her, and sitting beside her was her sister. This was the first time she had laid eyes on each other in ten years. Lila stopped in her tracks, too scared to move for fear that Lisa would disappear. Lisa was still as beautiful as ever. Her hair was hanging with just a little curl at the ends, and she wore a little lip gloss and her eyebrows were arched to perfection. She looked as if she was on her way to a country club. Her aunt looked up and stopped in mid-sentence when she spotted Lila. Lisa followed her gaze and leaped from her seat

"La-La! Oh my God, La-La!" The sisters grabbed each other and held on as if the other might disappear if they let go. Barbara dabbed at her eyes as she watched her nieces embrace. Lisa was the first to let go. She pulled Lila to the seat next to her aunt and took tissue from her purse and dabbed at Lila's face.

"We can't just be crying all up in the airport." A little old lady sitting in the corner turned towards Lisa and shook her head and mouthed, "Yes you can." Lisa smiled and grabbed Lila's hand.

"Lila, I have been praying for this moment for years. Now both of my favorite people are here. Let's go to the house so we can catch up," Lisa said as she gathered her aunt's small bags.

Lila wondered what she had done to deserve a second chance.

Lisa's fiancé, Darren, was waiting in the car when they got outside the airport. Lisa made the introductions while Darren packed their luggage in the trunk. Lila was so overwhelmed that she was speechless.

"Okay Lila, you're too quiet. Is there something wrong?" Barbara asked before Lisa and her fiancé got in the car.

"There is nothing wrong, Auntie. I just have a lot on my mind. Darren seems nice. I hope he's good to her," Lila whispered.

"Lisa's not the type to take much off anybody. You should remember that. She was the one fighting your mother when she didn't do what she was supposed to do for you girls. Remember?" Lila did remember.

"One time Betty forgot to sign a permission slip for you to go to the zoo, and if it weren't for Lisa, you would have missed that trip. Lisa sat right by your mother until she finished writing the note and signed it. Lisa took you by the hand and walked you right back to that school and turned it in to the office before they closed. I was so glad that the school was across the street from the house. I believe if it was on the other side of town, Lisa would have walked anyway."

"I remember that. That was first grade and I was crying because I didn't have my note by the end of school. Betty promised to walk it over but never showed up. I cried to Lisa, and I remember her saying, "You won't miss that trip." Lila smiled.

Lisa was her guardian through all of the bad times, and when Lisa was taken away by her father, Lila had been left to fend for herself. What would her sister say if she knew the kind of life she had been living since they were separated? Lila didn't want to do or say anything to make Lisa ashamed of her.

CHAPTER 31

By the time they got inside the brownstone and sat down to rest, guests had started to arrive. Lisa had invited the bridal party over to meet her family. Lila was a little hesitant at first, but with her aunt by her side, she knew she would not feel left out and so she joined the little party. She made up her mind to have a good time. Angel, one of the bride's maids, pulled Barbara and Lila to the side and told them that they were surprising Lisa with a bridal shower at their favorite restaurant, Jach's, at five-thirty the next day. Lisa thought they were all meeting for dinner after the rehearsal. Angel told her that they had purposely waited so that Lila and Barbara could be present.

"I thought we missed the bridal shower. I'm glad they waited for us," Barbara said.

"That was nice of them. Lisa has good friends, and look at all she has accomplished, Auntie. There are plaques and trophies for running track in high school, awards from her job, and she even has some volunteer awards too. She really blew up after she left us."

"And when you look at your accomplishments, you should feel proud too. You've done outstanding things to come back from your childhood, and I'm sure Lisa is as proud as I am that you did. Now let's go up to our room and put our clothes away. We especially need to hang up our gowns or we'll look a mess on Saturday.

"I'll let Lisa know we're skipping out," Lila said, waving to get Lisa's attention. Lisa moved over to where Lila stood and wrapped her arms around her.

"You don't know how much I prayed for this day. You and I are inseparable from this moment on. You got it?" Lisa said, squeezing her sister.

"I got it. Now go be with your friends. Auntie and I are going up to our room."

An hour later, Lila woke up to hushed voices in the bed beside her. Lisa and their aunt were chattering away in whispers about something, but Lila could only make out a little of what they were saying. She sat up and stared them, and when they saw that she was awake, they looked as if they had just got caught stealing.

"What's up?" Lila asked, looking at the two conspirators.

Lisa spoke first. "Betty called and said she heard about the wedding and was hurt that I had not invited her. Can you believe that? I haven't heard from her in at least a year. I know Aunt Caroline told her that I was getting married and she wasn't invited. You know how messy she is."

Lila knew exactly how messy Lisa's father's sister was. She was constantly over at their house when they were growing up, constantly meddling in their business. The fact that Betty and William were no longer together did not stop her friendship with Betty.

"I invited her Lila," Lisa said without emotion. She looked at Lila, pleading for her to understand.

"Is she coming alone?" Lila asked.

"No."

"How much are their tickets and the hotel fee. I'll pay for it. I don't want you spending money. This is your special time."

"Neither one of you is paying for it," Barbara said. "I'm paying. I've already talked to Betty. I also told her she better not come here with no attitude or drama or she'll be out on her you-know-what with you-know-who sitting on the sidewalk with her!"

Lila began laughing uncontrollably. She thought about her mother and Craig being bounced down the steps of the brownstone, Craig holding onto his SSI check and her mother holding onto Craig. What a sight.

CHAPTER 32

The cab pulled up to the curb, and Barbara, Lisa and Lila watched Betty and Craig emerge from the taxi. Lisa had gotten the phone call that their plane had landed and she had instructed them to come to the house for breakfast. She said that Darren would drive them to the hotel when they were ready.

"Lisa, this is your show. You go out and greet them. That'll give me time to prepare for her insults," Lila said, now leaving the window and sitting down at the kitchen table.

"Like I said yesterday, there will be no drama on this trip or somebody is getting put out!" Barbara said as she turned on the stove so she could make pancakes. Betty always made a loud entrance, and today was no different from any other.

"Oh Lisa, I knew you was going to be somebody. Look at all my baby's stuff, Craig. I told you my kids was special." Craig bobbed his head up and down and grinned, showing yet another gold tooth that was added since Lila had last seen them.

"Lila, you don't see yo' mama entering a room, girl?" Lila got up to give her mother a quick hug. Amazingly, she didn't smell like cigarettes and she was dressed decent enough. Her micro-braids were done neatly and pinned into a bun, and she wore a brown leather suit with brown boots. The skirt was a little too short for Lila's tastes, but she had to admit that her mother looked better than she ever had. Craig had on a gray leisure suit he saved from the seventies and a pair of gray loafers. His Jeri curl was as wet as ever, but he had it shaped around the edges. Bonnie and Clyde had come up in the world. Then Lila remembered that her aunt had sent them money. She knew her aunt probably sent more than she had told Lila and Lisa so Betty wouldn't come to New York and embarrass her daughter on her wedding day. She gave her aunt a knowing look and sat back down at the table.

"Hello ladies," Craig said, and he joined them at the table. Darren and his father and mother were on their way to the house to meet the family and to have breakfast. The doorbell rang again, and Lila put her head down when the door opened. It was Lisa's father, William.

"Hello, Daddy. Where's my mother?" Lisa said, hugging her father and searching for her stepmother. Her stepmother was an exceptional woman and had been an exceptional mother to Lisa, raising her as if she were her own daughter. She alone could take credit for guiding Lisa through her difficult years before adulthood. Lisa grabbed Jennipher and hugged her tightly.

"How's my baby girl doing?" Jennipher asked, stepping back to look at Lisa.

"I am on top of the world, Mother. My sister is here. Did Daddy tell you?"

"Yes, and I'd like to meet her," Lisa motioned for Lila to come over.

"I want you to meet my mother, Lila." Betty looked at Barbara and started to say something, but Barbara glared at her as if to say, "Don't even try it."

"Lila, this is my mother and best friend Jennipher."

Jennipher embraced Lila as if she was her long lost friend. "It is so good to finally meet you, Lila. I have heard so much about you from your biggest fan over here. You are just as beautiful as your sister. Are you enjoying yourself?" Jennipher asked, smiling benevolently at Lila.

"I am. I didn't think I would be comfortable around so many new people, but it's been fun."

Jennipher stepped aside and gave her husband a stern look. "Hello, Lila. Glad you could make it." William extended his hand. Lila shook it and went back to the kitchen table. She had survived the moment she had dreaded for weeks. She'd had visions of Lisa's father insulting her like he did when she and Lisa were young.

"Lila, start filling those hot trays with food so we can get this party started right," Barbara said, handing Lila plates of pancakes, pan-fried potatoes, biscuits, bacon and sausage. William and Jennipher finally made it to the kitchen where Betty and Craig sat transfixed by the food as if they hadn't eaten in months.

"Mother, this is Betty and her friend Craig," Lisa said, pleading with her eyes for Betty to go along with her introduction and not make a scene.

"Hello. It's nice to meet you, Betty and Craig," Jennipher said, extending her hand to the duo. They shook hands and nodded at the elegant woman standing before them.

"William, you gone say hi or just stand there gawking," Betty said with her hands on her hips. She smiled at William as if he had missed out on some great thing.

"Hello Betty, and nice to meet you Craig." William and Craig did the famous male handshake and stood awkwardly by their mates as if they needed permission to do something else.

"Hello to all of ya'll. Now come on and eat this food people. My feet hurt," Barbara said, and she motioned for the small group to form a line for the sumptuous food she'd prepared.

When everyone was seated, the doorbell rang again, and Darren and his mother and father joined the group at the table. Darren introduced his parents and then joined the group at the buffet-style breakfast.

Lisa was amazed at how well behaved Betty was during their meal. She hadn't picked a fight with her daughters or with William. Lisa tapped her juice glass with her fork, signaling that she had something to say, and everyone looked up from their plates to listen

"I would just like to say that Darren and I are honored that you all have come here to witness our covenant with God and one another, and we have a small token of our appreciation for you in the living room. It doesn't matter which bag you take. They all have the same thing in them. Darren, would you like to add anything?" Lisa said gazing at Darren and smiling.

"I would just like to thank Lisa's parents for all the time and money they have spent on this wedding, and most of all, for the beautiful person that stands by my side." Darren turned and kissed Lisa on the cheek and they sat down together.

Betty looked at Barbara and rolled her eyes. Lila could almost read her mind: William and that Jennipher person were taking all the credit for the daughter she had carried nine months in her womb.

"Lisa did you tell your family that you are going to be a doctor soon?" Jennipher said proudly.

"No I did not, Miss talk-a-tia, but you just did." The small ensemble cried congratulations almost in unison. Lila almost leaped out of her chair.

"You didn't tell me you were studying medicine, Lisa?" Barbara said, looking at Lisa with a pleased expression.

"I didn't think about it, Auntie. I was so happy to find you guys, it just slipped my mind."

"Being a doctor slipped your mind?" Lila said. "You must be in love, 'cause I would have told everybody that." Lila laughed.

"I know, miss chatter box. You couldn't hold one secret unless it involved getting some candy to keep quiet." Lisa laughed. She thought about the times she had to bribe little Lila with candy so they wouldn't get their tails tore up by her Aunt Caroline when she would baby-sit. They would have an opportunity to talk about old times and new things as soon as their guests were tucked into their beds for the night. Lisa told everyone to make themselves at home while she said a few words to

Darren. This would be the last time they saw each other until they said their vows. Darren would drop Betty and Craig off at their hotel before he and his parents went back to his place.

"Well Doc, this is it until tomorrow. You promise to come down that aisle at thirteen hundred hours, right?" Darren asked, pulling Lisa close to him.

"Wild horses couldn't keep me from walking down that aisle. Did you see how good everybody is getting along? I swear I think my Auntie Barbara paid my mother dearly to act right."

"Come on, Doc. You never know. Your mother might have really changed. She looks pretty good to have an old kid like you." Darren laughed.

"Oh, so I'm old now. You want me to meet you tomorrow, right.?"

"You know I love old women." Darren ducked before Lisa's fist connected with his head. "Anyhow Doc, I'll see you in church tomorrow. Sweet dreams.

"I love you," Lisa said sincerely.

"Not more than I love you, Lisa."

CHAPTER 33

Barbara and Jennipher sent everyone their rooms while they stayed downstairs to clean up. Barbara and Jennipher had become fast friends. They chattered as they washed dishes. Barbara felt bad that her own sister had decided to go to the hotel rather than stay and clean up with her. They had always cleaned together when they were teenagers. So much had changed since their youth. She missed her sister, but no matter how hard she tried, they never went back to the way they were. She prayed that Lisa and Lila could find their special bond again. Sisters should be close.

"Finally, we have time for just us. Lila, you are so pretty. You look just like your mother used to look back in the day."

"You look more like your mother than I do," Lila said, smiling. She lay down beside Lisa and folded her arms under her head.

"Oh what I wouldn't give to see the look on old Mrs. Randall's face right this minute. I'd walk right up to her snooty behind and say, 'Did you know that one of the ragamuffins is going to be a doctor? Do you have a P-H-D? Did you even finish high school? Oops, sorry, interview over. Be Gone!'"

"Ooh Lila, that is not nice. You're supposed to be the nice one." Lisa laughed when she thought about Mrs. Randall with that tight bun and tight face. She turned around on her side, propped her head up, and made a face like Mrs. Randall used to.

"You just as fass as you used to be, girl. I'm gon' tell Betty the minute she get back from them streets, ya hear me," Lisa said, doubling over with laughter.

"You look just like that crazy lady, girl. Oh God we gotta stop this. Mrs. Randall might show up here. You know how much Betty loved that lady. I never understood their relationship," Lila said.

"Betty loved anybody who would watch her kids and give her food stamps or money. Remember how we used to eat at Mrs. Randall's house or go over and get some can goods or milk?"

"Yeah. I guess she was okay in her own way. She just didn't like us," Lila said, shrugging her shoulders.

"Okay now. What's going on in your life La-La. Who is this Samuel person?"

"Samuel is a dream, Lisa. I couldn't have asked for a better man. He's very tall and sexy, but best of all, he's treated me like a real lady since the day I met him. You should see the kind of work he does. He's a contractor and builds houses, and he remodels them too. There's just one thing. He's a devout Christian and doesn't believe in sex before marriage. Can you believe that in this day and age?"

"Yes, I can. Some people live like that. Me and Darren aren't like that, though I know we should be. Pastor Williams would say 'shame, shame' if he knew what I was doing, but that's how I'm living. Remember, we used to take the bus to church every Sunday because of the treats?"

"I do. You used to give me some of your candy sometimes when we didn't have enough foo..." Lila stopped herself.

"It's okay to remember, Lila, even the bad stuff. We're past that now. I hated being poor and hungry too, but we had each other. It's over now. Now we'll step into the future and experience new things. We'll have children and watch them grow up with each other. You'll see. Better days are ahead, La-la."

CHAPTER 34

"Surprise!" the crowd yelled when Lisa entered the room. Lisa screamed with joy. They had played her good. She thought she was having her party after the wedding, but they had flipped the script on her. The private room at Jach's was filled with all her favorite dishes and some of the house specials. Crystal dishes with creams and sauces were placed beautifully on the white table cloths, and the room was decorated in pink and white, her favorite colors. She was a member of the Breast Cancer Awareness Committee at the hospital she worked for, and those colors represented something very dear to her. She knew her best friend, Tarah, had planned the festivities.

All of her female friends and family were present and accounted for. Betty was even glowing in her off-white sweater dress and pink boots. Lila knew that somebody must have gone shopping with Betty. She had never seen her mother dress so nicely. She had taken her braids down and they flowed as she moved toward Lisa.

"I cain't believe you studying medicine and all. You did real good for yourself, Lisa. Your man look like he doing good too," Betty said, keeping her distance so Lisa wouldn't make a run for it.

"You look better than I've seen you look in forever. Is Craig the reason for your sudden change?"

"Craig is good. I cain't run the streets forever, girl. He showed me some new thangs to do with myself. I volunteer sometimes, just like you do."

"I'm glad for you. Are you and Aunt Barbara close again?"

Betty put her head down. "My big sister is too big for her britches. She always trying to run my life. I'm grown now."

"That's what big sisters do. If I'd had the opportunity to be with Lila, I would have been all in her business too, but only because I love her. Aunt Barbara loves you. Look at what she did with Lila. She has an education, a great job, and Auntie even put money in a savings account for her. That's more than y…"

"I wondered how long it'd take for one o' y'all to say it. I was sick when I was raisin' you and Lila…"

Lisa put her hand up to stop Betty. "You were not sick. You were an addict. You chose to live in a drug-induced state. Aunt Barbara and my father chose to love us."

Barbara and Betty noticed things getting heated between Lisa and Betty and moved to the door quickly so they could intervene if necessary. Barbara knew this day was coming, but she had not expected a confrontation at Lisa's shower. She moved so fast that mother and daughter were stunned when she got between them.

"Let's go over and enjoy the party, ladies. Barbara pulled Lisa and Betty to where the guests were waiting for the guest of honor to mingle with them. She knew Lisa had a lot to get off her chest, but Jach's was not the place to do it. Tarah was on Lisa's other side in a flash.

"Okay Lisa, sit in this special chair and wait while your maids and matrons present you with your gifts." Tarah was visibly relieved when Lisa followed her lead. She knew how Lisa felt about her mother abandoning her and Lila, but she didn't want Lisa to be embarrassed by what might happen between. She winked at Lisa when she was seated and began to call the names on the presents. The air was thick with the unfought battle between mother and daughter. It was only a matter of time before the battle became a full-fledged war.

CHAPTER 35

The room was cold and dark. Lisa could not sleep, no matter what she tried. She eased out of bed, slipped downstairs to the family room, and started a fire in the fireplace. It was only five-o-clock in the morning, but her sleep had been interrupted so many times it was no use trying again. As the fire blazed, Lisa recounted the encounter with her mother the day before. She had no idea that she was still feeling abandoned and hurt. Her step-mother had adopted her and treated her as if she had birthed her, but she still needed the love of her own mother, which surprised her. Betty was not the loving type, however, unless you were tall dark and of the male persuasion.

"Hey lady, you should be in bed getting your beauty sleep," Lila said, cuddling up next to Lisa on the couch.

"Good morning. And you should be resting, La-La. You have a long trip ahead of you tomorrow. Darren picked up Samuel already. He got in late last night. Darren said he could stay with him. I told him how special Samuel was to you, so he said he'd be more than happy to lend a bed to a fellow soldier."

"Thanks." Lila rested her head on Lisa's shoulder, and together they watched the fire, each lost in their own private thoughts. It was good to be near her sister again. She made a secret vow to be close to her sister just like she was when they were together.

"I'm sorry about yesterday. I thought I was over all that misery, but I guess I'm not. Maybe I should get some therapy," Lisa said softly.

"Well, if *you* go, I need to go too. God knows I could use some kind of therapy," Lila volunteered.

They both busted out laughing at the same time.

"She just makes me so mad, walking around like her stuff don't stink and thinking everybody should be grateful she even exists," Lila said.

"She thinks we owe her. She borrowed two hundred dollars from me and hadn't even called me in a year or more. I told her to keep it. I didn't want any more of her interruptions in my new life."

"I should be jumping for joy right now. I'm walking down the aisle with the love of my life, and I had a very good childhood after I got over the first part. You know I begged my stepmother to go back for you, and she did, but you guys had moved. That broke my heart. We were going to bring you back and then tell Daddy after you were already living here."

Lisa smiled at the thought of what her stepmother was willing to do for her."

"She must be a real special lady. Auntie Barbara found me, and like you, things were good after I got over the first part. After I met Samuel, I didn't want to be broken anymore. I embraced the new feelings I found with him, and I said yes to life, Lisa. Now I feel like a brand new person."

"Me too. Darren has been so patient with me, and very understanding. I told him everything. I don't want any secrets or misconceptions about who I am. But guess what?"

"You're pregnant."

"Get your mind out the gutter, little sister. Our first duty station is Fort Irwin."

"Where's that?"

"About three hours from where you live, dodo bird."

"YES! Now it can be like old times." Lila knew now that God really was listening to her prayers. Maybe it was time she listened to Him. He sure had her ear now. Samuel told her that, if she believed, anything was possible. She had trusted his advice and put it into practice, and now she could see the changes taking place.

"Now I know you two are not sitting here like nothing is happening in a couple of hours. Ya'll better get to bed," Barbara said, staring at the sisters as if they had lost their minds.

"Don't get your panties in a bunch, Auntie. We're okay. I couldn't sleep, and Lila and I were talking about getting some counseling or something. We gotta get Betty out of our system."

"Good luck. I tried that for years, and the heffa ain't left yet." They all busted out laughing.

"We are pitiful, but we're together again. Lisa's moving to California when they get back from their honeymoon. Have you ever heard of Fort Irwin, Auntie?"

"No, but I heard of 'get somewhere and go to sleep so Miss Lisa can look like a bride and not a bat.' Now get!"

"Dang! Who woke her up?" Lila whispered, pulling Lisa back up the stairs.

"I heard that little woman! Never mind who woke me up. Get ta moving up them stairs." Barbara started after them, and they hit the stairs running. She remembered the summer she was able to keep them and how much joy they had added to her life. Both girls had overcome adversity and were moving into new and exciting paths. "If only Betty could feel something for her daughters," she thought.

CHAPTER 36

The church was decorated with maroon and pink floral arrangements, and on each side of the entrance to the church, maroon velvet drapes were pulled with a four strand pearl clasp. Small floral arrangements were on each end of the church pews. There was a balcony on both sides of the enormous church decorated with the same floral arrangements that adorned the pews. Lisa said the wedding was going to be big, but Lila thought big was not the word for this wedding. She didn't know enough people to fill one pew let alone the whole church. The security was so tight at the front gate that she wondered if Lisa and Darren were celebrities and forgot to tell her.

The wedding wasn't set to start for another hour, so Lila had asked Samuel to meet her in the church so they could talk before the ceremony. Samuel stood in the doorway of the church, watching Lila touch flowers and gaze around at the decorations for a few moments before he interrupted her.

"Are you real or are you a figment of my imagination?" Samuel said as he entered the sanctuary. Lila turned to see who was speaking even though she already knew.

"Come see," Lila said, holding her hands out for Samuel. He grabbed her hands and pulled her towards him.

"I missed you, Samuel. How long has it been since we saw each other?"

"Three weeks. Way too long." Samuel stepped back to get a good look at Lila. . "You look gorgeous. I can't wait to see you in your gown."

"You don't look too bad yourself. I'm glad Darren didn't mind you walking with me. I wouldn't want to walk with anyone else."

"You never had to worry. I was destined to be your mate, love." Samuel planted a quick kiss on Lila's cheek. We better go back to our places and get ready. I love you, Lila." Samuel left a stunned Lila in the middle of the church. She hadn't been able to say I love you in return, even though she believed it was the truth. Lila went back to the dressing room to get dressed. Maybe she was like Betty. Maybe love was too hard for her.

PostPartum

*   *   *   *   *

Lisa was a beautiful bride. Her dress was the palest of pink and designed by one of Lisa's friends from college. At the end of the ceremony, Darren surprised Lisa with an imitation mink coat that had a train just like her wedding gown. She looked like royalty gliding out of the church and into the white limousine that waited at the front of the church. The rest of the wedding party entered the other limousines and followed the bride and groom to the reception hall.

It had started to snow, and the streets were covered in white as if New York knew a wedding was taking place and had laid out a white carpet. The bridesmaids were chattering among themselves, except for Lila. Her mind was still in the chapel where Samuel had declared his love for her. Every time he touched her in the church, and when he helped her into the limousine, her heart skipped a beat. She smiled and gazed at the beautiful flakes fall to the ground.

The wedding went without a hitch, and even Betty looked as if she really might cry. The true test was when they got to the reception hall and the alcohol started flowing. A little of the bubbly and Betty might go off like a cannon. Lila hoped her aunt was prepared to intervene if anything happened. She wanted to spend her time with Samuel. There would be lots of food and music, and she thought maybe that would keep the Bonnie and Clyde of the ghetto occupied.

CHAPTER 37

The reception hall was just as beautiful as the chapel had been. The tables held pink and maroon napkins on white tablecloths. The chairs were decorated in alternating colored chair covers with bows attached to the backs. There were tables that sat two, four, six, and the bridal table for Lisa and Darren. Balloons bearing the newlyweds names floated in the air. Lila, Samuel, Barbara, Betty, Craig, William and Jennipher sat together at one of the two tables that were reserved for the family of the bride. Darren's family was seated directly behind them. Everyone bobbed to the music as they waited for the bride and groom to make their entrance.

"Lisa was the most beautiful bride. Did you see that mink Darren had made to cover her? It was like she was royalty," Barbara said, smiling from ear to ear.

"I felt like I was in Hollywood or something," Lila said.

"Well, I'm still the luckiest man in the room. Lila, you look like a million dollars. I couldn't concentrate on the ceremony with you so close," Samuel said, covering Lila's hand with his.

"Lila ain't never been as pretty as Lisa. Lisa's a beauty for sure. Lila just bright with that straight hair and everybody always took to her 'cause uh that." Lila wanted to run from the table, but Samuel had a firm grip on her hand; and when she looked at him, he smiled as if he knew what she was thinking. Betty just sat at the table as if she had just said the food was great. Nothing seemed to faze her.

"Lila is more than a bright girl with straight hair. She's beautiful. Maybe you were too busy to notice," Samuel said sincerely.

"Both of my nieces are gorgeous. They look a lot like our mother. Lila even has one dimple like our mother."

"I think you got two pretty girls Betty," Craig said, grinning like a loon.

"I ain't saying Lila ain't nice looking, but Lisa is the beauty. Lila ain't got no man trying to marry her." Lila jumped up, mumbled something about going to the bathroom, and left the table in a hurry. Barbara got up, glared at Betty, and followed Lila. She caught up with her in the bathroom.

"Lila, don't let Betty spoil the night. You know she's always sayin' something stupid. She just does these things because she knows she'll get us all worked up. Lisa and Darren will be here in a minute. Take a minute and get yourself together, and then come back out and sit with your man. Just smile and nod at Betty. When they start pouring champagne, she'll forget all about you, and everybody else."

"Thank you, Auntie." Lila kissed her aunt on her cheek and went into the bathroom to splash water on her face to calm herself down. Lila didn't care what Betty acted like as long as she didn't expose anything embarrassing to Samuel. She just needed to make it through the night, and then she could start the rest of her life off right.

When Lila turned to leave the bathroom, she felt as if the room was spinning and had to hold on to the wall for support. "I'm making myself sick with all this nonsense," Lila whispered to herself, and once she got her bearings again, she hurried back to the table before the room started to spin again. She sat down and smiled as if nothing had happened. "Just a couple of hours," she thought, as she watched for Lisa to make her entrance.

CHAPTER 38

The weather was unseasonably warm in California for February. The birds were singing and the sun was shining as if it were a warm summer day. A cold chill went up Lila's spine in spite of the weather. She thought of the saying her mother used when she was spooked about something. "Somebody done walked across my grave," she would say when she got a cold chill or felt scared. Lila felt as if someone had poured ice water into her veins. She couldn't understand why she was feeling so spooked.

The wedding and reception had gone as well as could be expected given Betty's presence. After Betty's insult to Lila at the beginning of the reception, she had calmed down and drank champagne and ate food like it was going out of style the whole night. Craig wasn't too far behind her. The two of them ate enough to feed at least ten people.

Lisa was glowing and happy as she made her exit for the honeymoon. The bride and groom both looked as if they had finally completed a lifelong journey of some kind and were now being rewarded. Lila wondered if all marriages started out like that, the bride and groom excited and happy to be together before the everyday hassles of life caused them to see each other in a different way. She'd heard it was much more to marriage than love, and she hoped she'd find out what else was needed before she took the plunge.

Samuel was the best thing that ever happened to her, but maybe she needed to learn what was required of a wife before she started thinking seriously about marriage. She definitely had to think about the church part. God knows she didn't want to end up wearing a long flowered dress and praising all day and night. She didn't want to raise kids who went to church but cussed you out when the church door closed — most of the church kids she knew were the biggest brats and caused the most trouble. Samuel would have to find someone else for that. The phone rang and jolted her back to reality.

"Good morning, beautiful. I know you're there even though you haven't said anything." Samuel then waited on her reply.

"Oh...Samuel, what's up?" Lila said.

"I think the question is, are you up? You sound out of it. Is everything okay?"

"I just woke up on the wrong side of the bed, Samuel. Give me a few minutes and this fog will pass."

PostPartum

"Okay then. Listen to this. I'm coming to California again to help a partner of mine who is building in a small town right next to Juniper. I'll be there for three weeks. Do you think you can handle seeing me once or twice a week?"

"You know I want to see you. Maybe then we can see if we really want each other."

"I know what I want, Lila, but I know you have to decide if being with me is what you want." Samuel wasn't sure if Lila was ready for what he was offering, but he was determined to be patient and wait. God never steered him wrong.

CHAPTER 39

Andrew sped down the freeway toward Charlie's Chrysler, the car dealership that had promised him a good deal on a Sebring. Angie had fallen in love with a black Sebring convertible she'd seen on the internet, and she bugged him until he had finally given in and started looking around the dealerships for a deal. Angie was so excited about the new car that she hadn't noticed her phone vibrating in the cup holder in the middle of the front seat of the Jeep.

"You may want to answer that, unless it's someone you don't want to talk to."

"Oh shoot. I didn't even notice I had a call. I forgot to take it off of vibrate." Angie snatched the phone up, but it had already stopped vibrating. She flicked the top open to see who was calling her. Her friend Jay's number was on the screen just before it stopped vibrating. She hit redial and called Jay back. She didn't hear the phone ring before Jay was on the line again.

"Girl, Tarzan is down at the Chicken Shack telling everybody how you dumped him and went back to your husband. You better figure out how to shut his mouth. He didn't say your name yet, but somebody gonna put two and two together in a minute."

"Slow down, Jay. Who are you talking about? Who is this Tarzan?" Angie was searching her brain for someone she could have ditched in the last year.

"Don't be so slow, Angie. Tarzan, you know: tall, white and buff — the workout guy you was playing with before you decided to make your marriage work."

"Oh God, when did he get..." Angie forgot Andrew was sitting next to her. He turned to stare at her when she suddenly stopped talking.

"Who is that on the phone?" Angie put the phone on hold.

"It's Jay. One of our friends is in trouble. It seems like something she can handle though." Angie pressed the hold button and heard Jaynell asking Tanya to keep it clean, whatever that meant. She had no idea that Jay was watching Tanya and Tarzan cry together, and Tanya had shoved her big butt so close to the man she might as well be sitting in his lap.

"Jay, is everything okay?" Angie asked praying that Josh had already gone home, or better yet, left with Tanya. She would go home with him and stay if he asked. If anybody could make a man do whatever she wanted, it was Tanya, who was very accommodating and very weak when it came to men. She had to admit that Tanya also had the measurements to break any man down. She was just country as hell. Whatever they wanted, she provided. Angie knew that Tanya was in between men, and she was hoping that Josh would make his new home with her.

"Girl, this country bama done broke your boy down. He is following her to the door like a whipped pup. You better pray he likes what Tanya has to offer. Call me when you get back home." Angie clicked the phone off and stared out of the car window. Her heart was beating like a drum. She turned to see if Andrew had gotten suspicious, but he was watching the Bentley that had pulled up beside of them.

"Everything okay?" Andrew asked then, as he watched Angie shift around in her seat.

"It seems like it," Angie answered, hoping that her words were true. Andrew turned and studied the Bentley again. I was obvious that something was up with Angie — he hoped it wasn't anything that would destroy what they had rebuilt together. A relationship could only take so much. Theirs had reached the limit.

CHAPTER 40

Lila felt dizzy as she slid off the side of the bed and onto the cold floor. Samuel had asked her to meet him for breakfast his first morning back in California and she had agreed. Unfortunately, her body was not cooperating with her commands. She gripped the wall and made her way to the bathroom right before she threw up in the sink. Lila turned on the faucet and rinsed the deposit from her angry stomach and hovered over the toilet until the nausea subsided.

Something was wrong. She couldn't keep her food down. Every morning for at least three weeks she had been throwing up. It was time to see the doctor. This was not a stomach virus as she had originally thought. Lila stumbled back to her bedroom and fumbled for the phone. She had to call Samuel and tell him she'd meet him for dinner. Mornings were no good for her lately. She dialed the number at the college and left a message for her supervisor. She hated to miss a day of work, but she could not go on the way she had been any more.

"Okay Samuel, please answer," she whispered as she dialed his cell phone number. It was only six in the morning, but she didn't want him to get up and start getting ready for no reason.

"Good morning, angel," Samuel said as soon as he saw her number on his phone.

"Samuel, I feel like crap. Can we meet for dinner? I'm making a doctor's appointment this morning."

"You want me to come over and sit with you. I can take you to the doctor's, Lila..." Lila cut him off before he could continue.

"No! I, uh, can do this by myself. I'll call you when I get back home. I'm going to lie back down now." Lila hung the phone up before Samuel could protest. All she wanted to do was lay back and rest until Doctor Smith's office opened at eight o'clock.

Samuel looked at the cell phone as if it had the answer to why Lila had hung up so quickly. He thought about going over to sit with her anyway, but she had told him no and he had to respect that. Maybe she had something that was contagious and didn't want to expose him to it. After all, he did come to California to work. His first meeting with his old buddy Manigault was at least three hours away. He decided to go to breakfast by himself. He'd save his proposal for dinner with Lila later.

CHAPTER 41

Andrew pulled the car into the garage and parked. Angie was out of the car before he could get the key out of the ignition. She took his hand gracefully and curtsied. He wrapped his arm around her waist and led her to the entrance of the dealership. The Sebring was spinning around on the showcase floor, and Angie squealed with delight like a child, bounded to the car, and ran her hand along the door.

"Andrew, I can't believe I'm going to drive away with one of these today."

"Let's find Allan and see if he has all the necessary paperwork. I hate spending a lot of time in dealerships. They always act like they're giving you this big deal when in reality they don't do much to reduce the price of the car."

"Don't be a party-pooper today. I'm happy, and you should be too. Now you won't have to drive the old car. You can drive the expedition, and I can cruise around in my sporty new Sebring."

Andrew asked the receptionist to page Allan so he could get things moving. He was glad Angie was happy, but he wanted to get back to Juniper before dark. He had promised his parents that he would take them to look at the new house he had purchased and take them to pick up their medications. This was one time he wished he had siblings. His parents were up in age, and he was the only one they could rely on besides his mother's sister Anna.

Anna was married and didn't come begging like his other family members. She was sixty, ten years younger than his mother, and still worked fulltime at the hospital in the neighboring town, Victorville. She came by once or twice a month to take his mother to the hairdresser or shopping for clothes. She also called once or twice a week to chat with his mother and to make sure things were going okay.

When he was growing up, there were lots of aunts and cousins who benefited from his parents wealthy lifestyle, but when his parents' health began to decline, so did the visits from their loving family. His father's family had never visited, and voices were hushed when anyone spoke of them. Andrew had only met his grandfather once, and it was over so quick he couldn't remember anything about him, except that he was a lot older than Andrew had expected and he was Caucasian. He remembered asking his father where his grandmother was, but the subject changed quickly. There were pictures of his grandparents on the mantel when he was growing up, but no one ever spoke of how they were or why they didn't visit.

He could only guess that his grandmother was not his grandfather's wife, but rather, his mistress. He had met the woman his grandfather said was his wife once, and she was just as white as his grandfather. There was no way the lady that was on the mantle was that woman.

He almost asked his grandfather about the woman in the picture, but his father had cut him off before he could finish the question, explaining later that he didn't want to stir up any bad feelings because his father was very sick at the time. Andrew figured there was more to that story, but he didn't want to upset his father and dropped the subject.

Andrew found out after his grandfather's funeral that his grandmother was a young girl who came to work with her mother in the kitchen of his grandfather's house. The young woman and his grandfather had an affair that produced two children, Andrew's father being the oldest. The two children were raised by their maternal grandparents and had never met. Andrew never knew if his father tried to contact his sister and hadn't gotten up the nerve to ask.

CHAPTER 42

Andrew sped down I-15 back to Juniper. He could see Angie in the rearview mirror. She was cruising along behind him, and he was glad the purchase of the car had gone smoothly. Now he had to beat it to his parent's house and complete that mission. Andrew found an easy way to keep Angie from going to his parent's house with him. He told her that his aunt needed him to do something and Angie probably would get bored waiting on him. Angie hadn't questioned him about what his Aunt wanted. She just told him to meet her at home for dinner. His mother still hadn't warmed up to his wife. They had been married for twelve years, and his mother still called Angie Miss Johnson.

Angie smiled when the passengers in passing cars looked over and smiled or nodded at her new car. She had never owned a new car and was overjoyed at the thought of her name being on the registration. She was getting personalized plates too. She couldn't wait to see Jay and Tanya. Before she finished that thought, she panicked. She had completely forgotten about the incident Jaynelle had called her about. It was a good thing Andrew was going to his parents. She needed to get home and call Jaynelle back and find out what happened.

Angie dialed Andrew on his cell phone. He picked up immediately. She needed to stop and get a soda. She was suddenly feeling nauseous. It was time to make an appointment to see a doctor. Angie knew the signs. Her body was changing, and there was no doubt in her mind why. She picked up her cell phone and dialed her doctor's number. She might as well see if she could get in.

CHAPTER 43

Lila checked in at the front desk of Doctor Smith's office and sat down to wait for her appointment time. She had already been to the lab and had her blood drawn. She flipped through the magazines on the table in front of her and found an old *Good Housekeeping* magazine. Her heart was beating so fast as she turned the pages without reading that she had to tell herself to calm down.

"Lila Williams," the nurse called out, looking around the room. Lila jumped up and went to the door where the nurse was standing.

"Please have a seat in the exam room on the right," the nurse said, smiling. Lila went into the exam room and sat down to await her fate. The nurse followed her inside the room and closed the door.

"Miss Williams, Doctor Smith had an emergency c-section this morning and won't be back until this afternoon. I apologize for the inconvenience, but we can reschedule you for this afternoon or you can see Doctor Taylor, who is covering for Doctor Smith, right now. She is a very good doctor."

Lila was a little upset. She knew Doctor Smith and would feel more comfortable seeing him, but she didn't want to wait until the afternoon to find out what was going on.

"I'll just see Doctor Taylor."

"Okay, great. I'm really sorry about this, but it happens a lot with OB doctors. Can I get you to roll up your sleeve and stick out your tongue?" Lila did as she was told. "My name is Katy, Lila. I talked to you this morning on the phone." Lila nodded. She was nervous and didn't want to talk.

"Just relax. Doctor Taylor is a really nice person as well as a great doctor. You'll like her." Katy took the blood pressure cuff off and flicked the thermometer cover into the garbage.

"You can just sit there until Doctor Taylor comes in. We have juice and some pastries in the front office if you want a little something to nibble on. It's my birthday and also my treat. Okay."

"Happy birthday, Katy. I think I'd like some juice." Katy said thank you and showed Lila where to get the juice. Lila took a small orange juice and a plain bagel and went back to the exam room. She nibbled at the bagel and sipped the juice. Her stomach wasn't as angry as it was earlier, but she took her time just in case things changed.

"Hello, Miss Williams," Doctor Taylor said as she entered the room.

"Hello," Lila said, trying to put down the juice and bagel to shake the doctor's hand. The doctor looked as if she had just stepped out of high school. She was five feet nothing if that, with pretty red hair that was very curly and tapered around her ears. She had on a pair of khakis and a tan and white shirt under her lab coat.

"Don't worry about getting up. Enjoy your bagel. Katy is feeding everybody this morning." Doctor Taylor went to the table, where she put down the record she had in her hand, and turned to Lila.

"Lila, I've looked at your labs this morning, and the reason you're feeling the way you are is because you're pregnant." Doctor Taylor waited for a reaction from Lila. She had learned quickly that pregnancy was not always a welcomed event for every woman.

"Oh God." Lila started to cry before she could catch herself. Doctor Taylor rolled her chair over and patted Lila's back.

"Are you okay, Lila? Does the father know?" Lila shook her head no.

"I can't have a baby, Doctor Taylor. I don't know anything about being a mother. The baby would be on its own, I can't do that to an innocent baby."

"Lila, we have parenting classes and a clinic right next door that specializes in helping new mothers. I could refer you, if that's all your worried about."

"No! You don't understand. I can't love. I don't know how. I just learned how to open up, and now I'm pregnant and it's not his baby and I can't…." Lila felt like she had said too much, even if it was all true. She didn't know what to give to a baby, and she didn't want to burden Samuel with a baby that wasn't his.

"Lila, let me get one of our counselors to talk with you. She's here today for group therapy and…" Lila cut her off.

"I don't want to talk in a group."

"That's okay. I'm going to ask her to speak to you alone. She's in my office right now using my computer, but she will be more than happy to speak with you. Her group sessions don't start until ten, so she has a little time. First, I want to talk to you about your test results. Your blood test shows you are a little anemic, so I want you to take more iron along with your prenatal pills. Here is a packet with all the instructions for the prenatal class that we offer and the schedule of tests and exams." Doctor Taylor handed Lila a plastic bag with a mother and baby on it that contained all the information she needed.

"The prescription for your prenatal pills and the iron pills are in that bag also. Take it to the nurse at the front desk, and she will call it in to the pharmacy for you. Just tell her which pharmacy you use."

"How pregnant am I?" Lila asked.

"From the last cycle date you gave us, you are about 12 weeks. Lila patted her stomach softly. There was a life growing inside and she needed to make a decision about what she should do. If she was anything like her mother, and she feared she might be, she couldn't possibly have a baby. She didn't want to put her baby through what she had been through. Maybe she could give her baby to her Aunt Barbara. She would love it and take good care of it.

"Lila I'm going to get Viola for you. Just relax and tell her everything. I saw your reaction when you found out how far along you are. I think this baby is very fortunate to have you. I wish you the best, and here is my card in case you decide to keep the baby."

Lila stood up to shake the doctor's hand and took the card. Doctor Taylor put her arms around Lila, gave her a big hug, and hurried down the hall to get Viola. Lila stood in the room with her hands around her stomach. How could she tell Samuel she was pregnant?

"Oh God, if you're listening, I need some guidance. I don't know what to do. I just don't know what to do. "What could the counselor say to her in such a short time that would be at all meaningful?" Lila thought as she waited for her to come into the room.

CHAPTER 44

Angie jumped up in bed and held on tight to her stomach. Andrew had already left for the office and she didn't know if her housekeeper was going to make it to work early. The queasiness and the dizziness just would not stop. She had to make an appointment to see her family practice doctor. Angie dialed Doctor Shaw's office number and waited while the recording told her at least fifty things that had nothing to do with why she called. The last message was important. Doctor Shaw had retired and there was someone new taking over her practice.

How could she leave without letting her know she was retiring? Angie thought about that for a moment, and then remembered she had received a card from Doctor Shaw but had tossed it on the computer to be read later. She was probably writing to tell her to find a new doctor and Angie hadn't even opened the card. She didn't know who else to call. Doctor Shaw had been her provider for most of her adult life. Angie dialed Jaynell's number to see if she knew of a good doctor. Shopping for a doctor was like shopping for clothes. You asked around until someone told you that the doctor they saw was the greatest thing since chocolate.

Dr Shaw had come highly recommended by her mother, but her mother was older now and was being seen by an internist. Jaynell probably could give her the name of a good doctor. She always had some kind of medical emergency when they were growing up.

"Hello! Hello!" Jaynell hollered into the phone.

"Oh I'm sorry, Jay. My mind is somewhere else this morning."

"Well, if you're worried about Tarzan and Tanya, you can rest now. Tanya is working him like a snake charmer. I went over to her mom's last night to see if everything was okay, and Tanya and her mother were waiting on lover boy hand and foot. I think he found his real family, girl."

"Well, that's a relief, but that's not why I called. My doctor retired, and I need to make an appointment with someone this morning. I'm not feeling all that great."

"Girl, dial nine, four, six, eight, two, four, six and tell the receptionist, Katy, that Jaynell sent you. Did you get too excited about the new ride?"

"No. I just feel tired and queasy. Maybe I need some vitamins or something."

"Maybe you need to pull yo' head out yo' ass."

"Jaynell, must you always be so vulgar. I just don't feel good. Now give me the number again and try to keep this on the low, low.

"Girl, you married. If you pregnant, you pregnant. You need to stop tripping and call Doctor Smith. I'll holler later. I gotta get to work." Jaynell slammed the phone down, making Angie's ear ring. Angie dialed the number Jaynell had given her and made an appointment for nine that same morning. She dragged herself out of bed and made it to the bathroom just in time to throw up in the toilet. She clung to the cool porcelain as if it could make the nausea go away.

"Oh God, please tell me I don't have this to look forward to for nine long months." Angie dragged herself to the shower, stripped, stepped inside, and turned on the warm water. She lathered her body with the complimentary lilac soap the bath shop had given her and started to feel like herself again.

Angie looked down at her stomach but didn't see much of a difference. The difference was in her sense of smell and the nausea she felt the first thing in the morning. That was one of the reasons she didn't want to have children — morning sickness and the fact that she may not get her shape back.

"Well, it is too late now," she thought. Angie accepted the fact that she was going to be a mother. She had not been sleeping with Josh long enough to know that Andrew was the father. Andrew had made it known he wanted to be a father from the moment they had met, but wasn't ready to tell him yet. "Candlelight and a dinner, and then, Bam! I'll give him the good news."

CHAPTER 45

Barbara folded the last shirt and put it in the drawer, and then she looked for her glasses so she could see the numbers on the phone. She was glad Leonard decided to come down and help Samuel with the new project. She wanted an excuse to check up on Lila. She knew her niece wouldn't mind her stopping in, but it was nice to have an excuse. Barbara knew that having Leonard and Lila under the same roof would be disastrous, and she was glad they could afford to stay in a hotel.

Lisa had called while on her honeymoon and made her promise to look in on Lila and to make sure their mother didn't get any more money out of Lila. Barbara had assured Lisa that she would check on Lila, and that, if Betty was anywhere near Lila, she would run her off.

Samuel called Leonard and set up a breakfast meeting with him since Lila wasn't feeling well. Barbara told the men to have breakfast in the room, and she would check on Lila. She had unpacked all of their things, and as soon as Samuel arrived, she left the men on their own.

Barbara drove the rental at top speed down the main street to the cutoff to Lila's apartment complex. Lila still didn't have a car even though she could afford one, but her niece was a miser. She saved every dime as if it would suddenly disappear if she didn't, which wasn't a bad concept. God knows, Barbara had blown enough money in her lifetime. She was proud when she thought about how well her nieces had done for themselves. She would give her right arm if her sister could see the blessings she had in her two girls just once.

Lila locked the door of her apartment and flopped down on the sofa. The plastic bag was still wrapped tightly around her wrist, and it was so tight that it had made a red welt. Lila was so distracted she hadn't realized how tight she had pulled the bag. She loosened the string and slipped it off her wrist and poured the contents of the bag on the couch.

Coupons for baby food, lotion, formula and other products littered the couch along with samples of baby lotion, wash and a newborn pamper. Lila picked up the pamper and marveled at how small a baby had to be to wear such a little item. She sniffed the lotion and baby wash and rummaged through the products to find the appointment card that the receptionist said was in the bag when she gave her the prescriptions.

The next appointment was in three weeks. Lila's eyes filled with tears again. She knew in her heart that she could never take the life of the little person growing inside of her. She had to take care of the baby and protect him or her from danger. She gathered the contents of the bag together and put them back in the bag. With tears pouring down her face, she tacked the appointment on her calendar, opened the spare drawer in her kitchen, and placed the bag of baby goods inside. The doorbell rang, and without thinking, she went to the door and flung it open.

"What's wrong, Lila?" Barbara asked stepping inside the apartment. If there was anybody she wanted to see at that moment, it was her Aunt Barbara, and she fell into her aunt's arms and cried her heart out. Barbara knew Lila would tell her everything eventually, but right now she needed a shoulder. She had come just in time.

CHAPTER 46

"Well, I can't say I'm surprised." Angie was now resigned to the fact that she would be a butterball in about eight months. Jaynell was right. Doctor Smith was not available, but Doctor Taylor was very nice and it was easy to talk with her. She explained everything and gave her a bag filled with information, prescriptions, and other things necessary for her journey into motherhood. Angie didn't want anyone to know about her pregnancy until she told Andrew, but there was one person she could confide in and with whom her secret would be safe.

Angie backed out of the parking garage and headed to her mother's house. She would make her mother promise not to tell her sisters because those two didn't care about secrets. They called their cousins and swapped information faster than the internet. Angie smiled as she thought about the new life growing inside of her. She wished her father had been able to see his first grandchild, but she knew it was because of his death that she had made an about face and pursued what was most important in life.

Her childhood home seemed smaller than normal, and though she had been back a couple of times after her father died, she still dreaded going inside for all the memories of him the place held. How could he not be there anymore? Angie gripped the steering wheel and the tears began to fall.

She thought she was over her father's death, but she obviously wasn't. She changed her mind about going in, turned the key in the ignition and started the car just as front door opened and her mother emerged in her gardening apron and gloves. She spotted Angie and a smile spread across her face.

"Angie, why you sitting in your car like that?" her mother said as she walked down the little path to the driveway. When she got closer, she realized why her daughter hadn't gotten any further than the driveway. She was still suffering. As Victoria opened the door, Angie shut off the car and sat limply in the front seat crying.

"Come on, baby. It'll get easier with time. Your daddy wouldn't want you crying all the time. Come inside and I'll slice you a piece of the pound cake I just took out of the oven. I swear, I should start a restaurant the way I have to cook around here." Angie followed her mother inside the house. Pound cake sounded good to her. The house smelled like fresh-baked goods. The smell brought back good memories of pound cake and ice cream sundaes.

Victoria sliced the pound cake and poured Angie a cup of coffee. Angie had pulled herself together enough to talk to her mother.

"Mother, I came over here for a reason. I thought I was over Daddy, but I guess I need more time."

"Everybody grieves differently. What did you want to talk about? Is everything okay?"

"I'm pregnant." Angie blurted it out without thinking. Victoria couldn't believe what she was hearing. Angie had sworn she didn't want any children.

"I can't believe what I'm hearing. I think I'm in shock," Victoria said as she stared at Angie in amazement.

"People change, Mother. Anyway, Andrew and I are excited about starting a family." Angie twirled the ends of her hair and waited for her mother's response.

"Okay, you're twirling away at them curls, so what else is going on?" She knew her daughter well. When she was a little girl, she always twirled her hair when she was only telling half of a story.

"Well, I want to wait until the right time to tell Andrew. I was going to plan a beautiful evening with wine and candles, so I don't want you to say anything to anyone until I tell you its okay."

"When you plan on telling him girl, next year at the baby's first birthday?"

"I just want everything done right. Can you just do that for me, Mother?"

Victoria looked at Angie and rolled her eyes. Young people were always waiting for the right time to do something. If she had of waited when she was young, something would have turned into nothing. Men always had a way of talking their way out of trying new things, at least her husband had. Dennis was old fashioned, and new things were dismissed with the old cliché: "If it ain't broke don't fix it." Victoria smiled when she thought of how many times she had heard that saying. She missed her old man at that moment.

"Okay Angie, I'll keep it quiet, but don't wait too long. I want to tell all my friends about my new baby. That's why you broke down in the driveway, isn't it? You always shared your news with Daddy first." Her mother had always called her husband Daddy just as Angie and her sisters had.

"Yeah, you know I love you Mother, but...."

Victoria waved her hand at Angie. "You don't have to explain that to me, baby. I know you love me, but you and your daddy had a special bond. He was so proud of you, no matter what you did, and not too many girls these days can say that. Now that you're grown and about to have your own baby, I can tell you this.

"Dennis had a baby girl with his high school sweetheart right out of high school. That girl and their baby burned up in a fire, and Dennis never forgave himself for not going over to her house that day. I think he relived that moment every day of his life until you made your entrance into the world. I'm not saying you took that baby's place, but he felt like he was given a second chance. He tried so hard to give you everything, and you made him very proud." Victoria smoothed the curl Angie had twisted back in place and kissed the top of her head.

"I feel so bad for Daddy. It must have been painful going through something like that." Angie placed her hand over her stomach and smiled. "I already love whoever this is. You guys gave me lots of love, and when this baby gets here, I'll make sure he or she gets what I got and more."

"That's my girl. Now you plan your little night with your husband real soon. I gotta spread the good news."

CHAPTER 47

Lila sat down on the couch opposite her Aunt and cleared her throat. She didn't want to tell her aunt she was pregnant. She tried to remember the positive things the counselor had said to her before she left the doctor's office, but nothing could take away the shock of being pregnant. She didn't even know how to start the conversation.

"I messed up, Auntie. I saw the doctor today and...I'm pregnant. I can't even tell you how bad I feel. I thought about having an abortion when I first heard the news, but I can't."

"Is that why you were crying so hard?"

"I was just feeling sorry for myself. I'm over that now. I have to tell Samuel. I'm sure he doesn't want to raise someone else's child.

"Lila, first of all I will be here helping and doing whatever I can, but you don't know what Samuel wants. Will you tell me who the father is?"

"I know who the father is, but I can't say. I got in this mess all by myself, and I'll deal with it by myself."

"Don't you think the baby has a right to know about the father? Will you keep it a secret from the child? Think about how you feel about not knowing your father."

"I haven't thought that far ahead yet, and as for Samuel, it's not fair to him to have to raise someone else's baby."

"Samuel knows about this man, doesn't he?"

"He does. I was honest with him, and he waited for me, but now look what's happened. I messed things up again."

"Don't be so sure about how things will go, Lila. Give Samuel a chance. You don't have to tell him about the pregnancy right now. It will be a while before you start showing. Keep seeing him so you can discover for sure if this is the man you really want. Then, if he proves to be that man, tell him about the baby and let him make up his own mind."

"I can't do that, Auntie. I don't want to feel the pain if he says he wants out."

"Pain is a part of life, Lila. Give yourself and this baby a chance at true happiness. I believe in my heart that Samuel will stay right by your side. He knew you were seeing someone, and he was willing to wait. Don't count him out yet."

Lila thought about what her aunt was saying. Could it be possible to keep her baby and Samuel? One thing was for sure. She was not choosing him over her baby. If he wanted out, it would break her heart, but her baby was number one from this day forward.

"Now, do you have any baby stuff around here or is it too soon?"

Lila jumped off the couch and went to get the bag she'd stuffed in the cabinet. She poured out the contents and together they went through everything. "Oh God, I forgot all about Lisa. She's still on her honeymoon. I'll tell her when she gets home."

"You do that. I never had no kids, but I swear I could have used some of this stuff when I babysat for your mother. They have a whole lot of nice things now. Don't give me that sad look. I wish you had of waited for the wedding before the baby, but it didn't happen that way and I'm still very proud of you. You could have gone to the clinic and ended this, but you didn't.

"I'm scared, Auntie. I think I may be like my mother, unable to love."

"That's where you are wrong. Betty loves that drug she's on. Nothing takes the place of that in her life. Don't take that personal. Addiction demands everything and gives nothing. Betty is actually dead already, and the only time she comes close to feeling anything is when the needle hits her arm and the drug flows through that needle into her veins. To her, that is life, but she really stopped living a long time ago. I don't know what triggered her downfall, but she's nothing like she was when we were growing up. She was top in her class, the best athlete, and voted most likely to succeed. I miss that person."

"I can't believe Betty did all of that."

Barbara had to take a deep breath so she could continue without getting emotional. "There was nothing Betty couldn't do. She played basketball like a pro. We all thought that she was going to college for basketball, but all of a sudden things took a turn for the worse. I think that's why our father died so early. He worried about her change so much. Our mother was a little different. She wanted Betty out as soon as she started messing up. Daddy wouldn't have it, but as soon as he was buried, Mama made Betty move in with Lisa's father's family."

"Maybe that hurt her. Have you ever asked her what happened?"

"Yes I did, but she just says, 'I made my bed and I'm lying in it.'"

"Oh. I feel bad for her now. Maybe she felt lost and didn't know what to do. She was pregnant with Lisa wasn't she?

"Yes, she was but something else happened. She wasn't the only high school girl pregnant. As a matter of fact, she wasn't even showing and finished high school without anyone knowing. Our mother knew, but she never discussed the subject. After high school, Betty went away for awhile and came back with Lisa."

"Did she say where she went?

"Nope, She just showed up in town at the Grocery Mart like nothing happened. She had her figure back and was stopping traffic as usual. That's when she began acting cold towards me. It was like I had done something without knowing it. We were never tight again. I miss my sister, Lila. I wish you could have known her then."

CHAPTER 48

Angie rushed inside the house and hid the bag of baby things in her closet. She couldn't wait until she sprung the news on Andrew. She dialed Jaynell's number and made herself comfortable on the bed.

"Who's yo' baby's daddy, girl?" Jaynell hollered into the phone.

"You need to stop playing Jay. You know Andrew is the father. Thank God. It could have easily been Tarzan, as you call him, but we stopped fooling around just in time.

"So congratulations. You know them curves you care about so much are going to disappear for awhile. Whatever will you do?"

"Jay, I swear I think you forget that you're my best friend sometimes. How could I possibly worry about curves when I'm carrying Andrew's seed."

"And it's because I'm your best friend that I know you trippin' about gettin' fat."

"I already know where to get clothes that accent your figure during this time, and I'm still cute."

"Now there's the girl I know, vain till the end. Okay, does Daddy Dearest know yet or are we waiting to spring it on him?"

"You know, I should call Tanya and see if she's excited about my announcement. Maybe she can come over and look at all the baby things and help me make some decisions. You seem a little too sarcastic today."

"You can call that bama if you want to, but she won't be leaving Tarzan's side anytime soon. Anyway, you know I'm happy for you girl, and I'll be there when you need me. I just asked if Andrew knew about the baby yet."

"No. I'm preparing a romantic evening for him Saturday. I'm going to tell him then."

"Okay. I'll be over there in a minute. I know you got stuff to show me, and don't go on and on about baby stuff. I got some gossip you need to know about."

"Well, bring it on, and I'll make us some lunch." Angie clicked off the phone and smiled. Jaynell always had some drama to tell her about, and it was always good gossip too, not some nonsense.

She kicked off her shoes, slid on her house shoes, and went downstairs to prepare lunch. Andrew didn't get home until six or seven usually. She had plenty of time to hear the latest gossip.

CHAPTER 49

Lila felt a little better after her Aunt left her apartment. She had laid everything out, and her Aunt was happy to help her. She still had the daydream where her mother would finally come around and apologize for everything, and then they would start all over, but she knew that was just a dream. There was still one more thing she had to do. Andrew needed to know that she was carrying his baby. She wasn't interested in causing trouble in his life, but she wanted the baby to know who the father was, which meant the father had to know he had a child. She picked up her cell phone and dialed his number.

"Lila, what's going on?" Andrew said, a little confused about why she was calling. She had made it clear to him that she had moved on with someone else.

"We need to talk, Andrew. Can you stop by after you leave the office today?

"What is this about?"

"Just come by for a second. It won't take long to hear what I have to say."

"Alright, but it won't be until eight or nine. I got some business to take care of."

"Okay. See you later, Andrew." Lila clicked the phone off and lay back on the couch. Growing up was much harder than she had figured. Maybe Betty couldn't handle all of the decisions that come with having a baby and that's why she turned to drugs. Lila shuddered as if a cold wind had blown across her shoulders. She never wanted to rely on a drug to help her with life. She'd seen the effects of the drug world firsthand and vowed never to tamper with that kind of evil.

Hours later, Andrew rang the doorbell, waking her out of a deep sleep. She went to the bathroom to check her face before she let him in.

"Lila, you look good as usual. What's up?"

"Have a seat, Andrew." Andrew sat down on the couch and Lila sat in the armchair next to him.

"This is really hard for me, especially after how we ended our relationship, but...I'm pregnant and you're the father."

"Now you been running around town with this new joker and you want me to believe that I'm the father of your baby? What's the matter? Did your man leave you?"

"First of all, we haven't slept together yet. He has high morals...."

"Oh really, and he's with you."

Lila let his sarcasm pass. His opinion didn't matter to her anymore. She had more important things on her mind. Lila exhaled and continued to talk. "Andrew, I'm almost four months pregnant. I know this is your baby. I seem to remember you wanting a baby badly. Remember?" Lila said staring at Andrew.

"That's when I knew you were with me and only me. Now you running this new brother and you want me to pick up the slack. What kind of game you playing here, Lila?"

"Andrew, I don't want anything from you. I haven't told my man yet, so I don't know what he'll say. I am just telling you that I'm having our baby. I thought you might want to know. It's simple." Lila stood up to lead Andrew to the door. If he couldn't understand that she was giving him the courtesy of knowing about their child, she didn't have anything more to say.

"So it's like that. You drop a bombshell, and when I don't jump for joy, you want me out."

"I don't want you to jump for joy. Actually, I don't care how you take what I've said. I thought I owed it to you and to the child to tell you. So, oops, there it is. I'm having your baby. I don't want your money, and I don't plan on telling anybody but my man about the baby's paternity. There will come a day when this child may want to know who you are, and I'm going to honor that request. I've taken up enough of your time, Your Honor. Thanks for hearing me out. Good bye!" Lila walked to the door, opened it, and waited for Andrew to exit her apartment. Half of the job was done. Now all she had to do was tell Samuel.

Lila felt a pang in her heart that brought tears to her eyes. How could she have been so careless with her birth control? She picked up the picture of her and Samuel that was taken at his sister's house and clutched it to her chest. Her carelessness had created chaos. She had to follow through with telling Samuel the truth. He deserved that. Her life had bloomed like a rose in springtime ever since Samuel stepped into it. Surely he'd continue to be her friend even if he couldn't bear the thought of raising someone else's child.

CHAPTER 50

Angie inhaled the sweet aroma of onions and the small steaks she'd grilled for lunch on her kitchen grill. Cooking the meals they had enjoyed so much during their college days brought back good memories. Jaynell and Tanya always preferred her cooking to any of the other girls in their apartment. It seemed like decades since she actually prepared a meal for anyone. Gayle did most of the cooking for her small household. She had forgotten how much joy she used to get out of preparing meals from the family cookbook her mother had given her.

The cookbook was one of the many gifts her mother had given her on her wedding day. It was a tradition to hand down the family cookbook to the bride as a gift. Angie had tasted a variety of the recipes in the book at family reunions and in her own mother's kitchen, and she had enjoyed them all. She'd helped her mother prepare meals until she went to high school and got on the fast track. Between boys and her other school activities, she hadn't had time to sit around and help with dinners. She suddenly missed those times with her mother. Surely she could have missed some games or practices to continue their tradition, but it was too late to dwell on those things now. She made a vow to cook with her mother on a Sunday at least once a month.

Jaynell honked the horn of her car before getting out and ringing the doorbell. Angie smiled when she thought about all the times she had done that in front of her parents' house — it drove her father crazy. "Is that girl alright," he'd holler when he'd pull the curtain back and see Jaynell leaning out the window smiling. The memories of good times in her childhood home threatened to come flooding through her. Jaynell jumped out of the Nissan and met Angie at the door.

"Girl, I can smell them steaks from here. I hope you put one on for Tanya. You know she can smell food from miles away, and I told her I was on my way over here."

"Jaynell, I know how you are. I have enough food for all of us."

"What you mean you know how I am?"

"I knew you would call Tanya and let her know we were having something."

"Yeah, well if we don't love her, who else will? You know she's special."

"Just admit you love Tanya, girl. I sure do. She makes me laugh with her special slow self."

"Come on in and sit down, please." Jaynell came in and flopped down on the stool at the kitchen counter.

"Okay Angie, remember the young girl that used to work at City Hall for about a three months and her aunt used to live next door to my cousin Carlos?"

"Yeah. She was pretty nice. I didn't know her well though. Why?"

"Girl, she is pregnant and don't know who the daddy is. Can you believe that?"

"In this day and age, anything is possible. Who told you?"

"I have my sources. I think she may be pregnant by Joe. They used to be seen together all the time."

"Not Joe Fontano."

"Yeah Fontano. I even saw them together at the movies one night. Why you surprised about that?"

"Joe just doesn't seem like the type, but you never know."

Jaynell looked at Angie and shook her head. "Uh Uh, it's more than that. You didn't mess with that little boy did you?"

"He's not a little boy Jay, and get your mind out of the gutter, girl."

"You did, didn't you? Oh Lord, please help me understand this freak in front of me."

"Jaynell, please stop being so dramatic. Let's talk about something else. My husband can walk in at any time you know. Now change the subject quick before Tanya gets in here. You know she can't hold water."

"Okay, but you nasty. Little Joe Fontano, how old is he? Twelve? Naw, I'm just playin'."

"Keep it up Jaynell and you are going to hit the floor hard. My stomach is not big yet." Tanya was at the door when Angie turned to cut up the salad.

"Come on in, Tanya. Jaynell was 'bout to get bounced. Get the Kool-aid out the bottom drawer over there. The pitcher and sugar are on the table."

"I'll just sit here and watch the two of you work," Jaynell said while Angie sliced cucumbers and shook her head.

"Jay you been here all this time and you haven't done one thing, I know," Tanya said, pouring half the bag of sugar into the pitcher. Jaynell avoided kitchens like the plague and so the observation was not all that insightful.

"What I know is that I wash my hands before I start making stuff for other people. We don't know where your hands been."

"I'll bet you'll drink this Kool-Aid," Tanya said. Angie laughed. She knew Jaynell would drink the Kool-aid and eat everything in front of her. She never turned down a plate or a cup.

"Is this 'pick on Jaynell day,' sisters? Can't we all just get along? Love is in the air, ladies."

"Please stop! You're making me sick," Angie said, putting the finished salad in the refrigerator until the meat was done.

"Tanya, how is it going with Josh?" Angie asked

"Everything is going good. He understands me. You really did a number on him though. I should be mad at you, but if you hadn't done it, we wouldn't be together. He says we were meant for each other."

"How nice. Are you guys getting serious?" Jaynell asked, giving Angie a knowing look. Tanya seemed to love anyone who wandered into her path. She never saw bad in anybody, which frustrated Angie and Jaynell to no end, but that quality was also one of the reasons they loved her so much.

"It is getting pretty serious. He is the first guy that doesn't mind Mama being around. We're a regular family now." Tanya's mother, Ettie, was another recipient of Tanya's kindness. Ettie claimed to be disabled, but every other weekend she was on the bus to Las Vegas, ready to gamble away her meager earnings from the state. Tanya just said, "Mama has her little senior citizen trip to ease her mind." Jaynell knew firsthand that Ettie was living it up on the machines and at the bar. She didn't limp or drag her foot in sin city.

"Jaynell, leave her alone. I'm glad he found someone he could be with. You need a man, girl."

"I can do bad all by myself. I don't see one reason I should settle down and be miserable. I'll leave the man-drama to you two. I'm staying sexy and single."

"Famous last words, I used to say that, remember?" Angie asked as she turned the steaks over. The recipe book didn't call for turning, but she wanted the burn on both sides of the steaks before she took them off the grill.

"You got caught up in what Andrew could do for you. I think status meant more to you than your precious freedom. You got it twisted, sistah."

"You may be right, but now I think I'm on the right track."

"I hope so, Angie. For real," Jaynell said.

"Me too. You always had a big stomach for sex. Maybe you need some pills or something," Tanya said seriously.

"It's a big appetite Tanya, and she don't need no pills. She needs Jesus. Can't no pill fix the sickness that colored girl got "raht cheer" as my granny can say."

"Now ya'll gone and insulted me in my own house. I will be what I will be. Now let's get some plates and silverware so we can eat. Please!"

CHAPTER 51

Samuel pulled the chair out for Lila and went to the other side of the small table to sit down. The restaurant was cozy, and the music was easy listening, making the atmosphere cheery and bright. Lila sat still. She was trying to forget her morning and focus on her date with Samuel.

"You are awfully quiet tonight, Lila. Are you feeling better?"

"I feel much better. I think it was just nerves. It's over now. Let's eat." Samuel smiled and picked up the menu.

"Good. Have you ever eaten here? What's good?"

"I like their shrimp scampi. You can just about order whatever you like. Nate's food is good. I usually just get delivery. I've only been inside two or three times."

"Okay, then I'll have the porterhouse. What about you?"

"I'm going for the scampi." Lila was glad the morning sickness didn't last all day. She was starving. The waitress came over with a pen and pad ready to take their order.

"Hello, I'm Goldie and I'll be your waitress tonight. Are you ready to order?"

"Yes. I'll have the porterhouse with fries. The lady will have the shrimp scampi." Goldie asked for their drink order and went to the kitchen to put in their order.

"Lila you have been very quiet tonight. Anything you want to talk about?"

"No, not really. I guess I'm just tired from this morning. How did your meeting with your friend go?"

"It went well. We have a lot of work to do in a little bit of time, but we're used to it. Manigault has a good thing going over there in Black Oak. If I was done with my business in Kansas, I would come out here and work for awhile, but I just can't make that move right now. So I'll help him out for a minute and then get back."

"You're a good friend."

"So is Manigault. He flew out to help me and Leonard when we first started Homes for Less. He's the best when it comes to floor plans and getting what the client wants down to the smallest thing."

"Do you miss the army?" Goldie came back with their drinks, and Samuel waited to answer while she set their drinks down and gave them each a straw.

"I miss some things, but I like my freedom. In the army, you are a soldier twenty-four seven. Weekends are not promised, and you always had to answer to somebody. But I went to college on their dime and was able to use my GI bill to buy my first home. I enjoyed that time, but I'm glad it's over."

"I thought about going in the army when I first got of high school. The recruiter was always on campus. He made the army sound like a paid vacation. All I had to do was join, go to basic, learn a trade, and then I could fly to exotic places and shop."

"You have to watch some recruiters. They'll say anything to get your name on the dotted line. I can't picture you in the army though."

"I can't either. That's why I didn't go. The first time I had to go to the field and get dirty, I would have been through." Samuel smiled. The restaurant started to get busy. He hadn't noticed the stage to the left of the entrance. Someone was on stage setting up microphones.

"Hey you didn't tell me they had live entertainment. This night is getting better and better."

"I had no idea. I never even noticed the stage. I wonder if that was there the whole time. I love live music too." Goldie returned to the table with their order. Lila laid her napkin on her lap and watched as Samuel did the same. She hadn't noticed that he had removed his jacket. She admired the body-fitting shirt he had on under the jacket. The muscles in his arms looked as if they would burst out of the shirt. His fine chiseled features brought the phrase "eye candy" to mind. She smiled and put her head down before he caught her staring. Sex was so strong on her mind that she could barely concentrate on anything else. "Aren't you already in a fix because of sex?" she thought. That didn't stop her from wanting Samuel in the prone position under her this very moment.

Lila forced her eyes off of Samuel and to the stage. The crew was bringing out the musical instruments and someone was doing a sound check. Samuel laughed and talked about his military days while Lila sat transfixed by the various emotions attacking her all at once. If he only knew what she was thinking.

CHAPTER 52

Andrew passed Jaynell and Tanya on his way back home. "Perfect timing," he thought. He didn't feel like hearing a bunch of cackling women in the house. Angie had left the Sebring out at the curb instead of putting it in the garage, and so after he pulled the Expedition into the garage, he went back out to the curb to move the car into the garage. He had a full day and wanted to eat, and then get into bed and get some sleep.

Lila was pregnant. That's all he needed right now, but she had said she would keep their secret until the child was old enough to know. That gave him plenty of time to establish a solid relationship with Angie. He had to admit that he was happy about the news, but he also hoped Lila kept her word. He pulled the car into the garage and closed it. He entered the house through the garage. It was quiet. Gayle had the weekends off, unless they had a function planned, so Angie was home alone.

Andrew saw the plate of food on the table. He lifted the foil and found the steak and potatoes. He opened the fridge to get a drink and found a vegetable salad on the first shelf. He got the salad and dressing along with his soda and laid them on the table. He went to the hall closet and stripped down to his t-shirt and slid on his sandals. Jaynell and Tanya had prompted his wife to do something that he had never been able to get her to do, cook. The kitchen was nothing more than a short cut to the garage for her until her friends showed up.

He was so tired and hungry that he didn't even look for Angie. He sat down to the meal and devoured it. He was taking the last gulp of soda when Angie appeared in the doorway. She walked over and sat down beside Andrew and took his hand.

"I had a wonderful time with my friends today. I feel brand new, Andrew. I think I've finally accepted that Daddy is gone, and I've discovered new things that make my life meaningful again. You got a minute?"

Andrew waited for the inevitable. Angie probably had the note in the pocket of her jeans. He could only imagine what Lila could have written. He hoped she hadn't revealed too much. "She couldn't be that dumb. Could she?" he thought as he waited for Angie to begin.

"I was going to plan a nice romantic evening with candles and a dinner, but I feel that this is the right time to tell you my news. You're going to be a daddy. I was a little suspicious when I started being so tired, but I wanted to be sure, so I had an appointment this morning. It's official." Angie smiled as if she had given birth already. Andrew couldn't speak. He was in shock. Angie had no idea what she'd just done to him.

"Wow! I don't know what to say after all these years," Angie started to worry. Maybe she had waited too long. He didn't seem happy at all.

"Is it too late, Andrew? What's wrong?"

"No, it's not too late. You just caught me off guard. Come here." Angie sat down on Andrew's lap. He kissed her neck and tried to recuperate from the shock. He had to convince Angie that he was excited before she caught on to his present mood. He rubbed her stomach and kissed it.

"I'm really happy, Angie. You know how much I wanted children. I'm just really tired, and you almost gave me a heart attack with that news. I never thought you'd want a baby."

"Things have changed, Andrew. We're going to start a family and act like a normal married couple. Let's not let your career or my clubs get in the way. Okay?"

"I promise not to let anything destroy our happiness." Andrew knew that was easier said than done now. He knew of one person that could shatter their lives if she wanted to.

CHAPTER 53

Lila slept like a log after her night with Samuel. His easy going attitude had allowed her to forget her troubles and enjoy a night out. Samuel had gone back to Black Rock to work for the week and would return to the hotel in Juniper for the weekends to spend time with her. She had made up her mind to do what her aunt suggested and follow through with the relationship until she was brave enough to share her secret with Samuel.

She'd already called her sister and broke the news to her. Lisa was overjoyed. She said she couldn't wait to be an aunt, and as soon as the army moved them to California, she would be her birthing partner. Lila did not tell Lisa who the father of her unborn child was and became very quiet when Lisa tried to pry it out of her. Too many lives could be destroyed if she revealed her secret now. One day, everyone would understand.

She was very busy working at the college, but she missed the small City Hall staff and her role as community clerk. She kept in touch with Joe, who filled her in on the happenings, but it wasn't the same. Lila logged on to her computer and waited while the programs she needed loaded. She made a mental note to make her next prenatal appointment. Being pregnant was still scary and strange, but she had committed to keeping the baby and so she had to make sure she ate right and otherwise took care of her health.

Lila had four students scheduled for a review of their classes so they could pay their fees and get a password for the college website. Working at the college had even prompted her to take classes towards a degree in Judicial Administration. Some good had come of her move along with the fact that she had kept her word to herself by ending her relationship with Andrew.

Several weeks later, Lisa's husband was transferred to Fort Irwin, but post housing was not available. On hearing that the couple had to move to Juniper until their name came up on the list, Lisa offered her extra bedroom to Lisa and Darren. Darren was reluctant at first, but after much begging and pleading from the sisters, he gave in. Lila and Lisa were ecstatic. Lila had gone through her apartment and cleaned as if the health inspector was making an appearance.

Her prenatal appointment had come up so fast that she hadn't been able to mentally prepare for it. Darren spent most of his time on post, and so she was able to voice her fears to Lisa. Lisa had calmed her when she was out of money.

The appointment went without incident, and Lisa was excited for both of them. She had bought a baby book and put the ultrasound film on the first page. You would have thought Lisa was the pregnant one. Lisa dragged Lila to the mall in Black Oak to window shop for a crib and baby clothes. Lila refused a baby shower, but she had agreed to go looking for the things she would need for her new addition. No matter how hard she tried, however, she could not seem to get excited about being a mother.

She was glad that the new styles were loose fitting. Everyone was wearing smocks and baggy T-shirts. Her stomach was beginning to show, and she wanted to camouflage it as long as she could. She was glad her relationship with Samuel was long distance at the moment. It was almost time to let him know what was happening.

Angie had to change her prenatal visit to accommodate Andrew's schedule. He had a video conference to attend on her original date, so she went a day early. He had surprised her by being utterly sweet and attentive during the whole process. She could even see tears in his eyes when the sonogram operator handed them the first picture of their unborn child. It felt good to have him by her side. They were on their way to their best years. She could feel it.

Angie couldn't say for sure, but she thought that whatever relationship he had with the letter writer had to be over. He had spent every moment that he wasn't at work with her. She had even attended a few functions with him when she wasn't feeling sick.

Andrew had spotted Lila and someone he assumed was her sister at the doctor's office. He'd heard through the grapevine that her sister's husband had been stationed at Fort Irwin. While being excited about the child Angie carried, he was still curious as to how Lila was doing with her pregnancy. Lila didn't see them because she was leaving the clinic when they came through the back door. "How could I go from no children to two on the way at the same time? Who could have planned something this bizarre?" he thought as Angie chattered on and on about names and birthdates. He was even more amazed that Angie and Lila ended up at the same clinic because Juniper had several clinics throughout the city. If he hadn't been so aggravated, he would have found his present situation comical.

CHAPTER 54

"Lila, Samuel has called at least five times this week. Have you had time to call him back?" Lisa asked as she washed the dishes they'd left in the sink from breakfast.

"Oh, uh, we're playing phone tag. I call him when he's not available and then he calls me. I'll just email him." She hadn't tried to call Samuel at all, but she was going to email him so he wouldn't get suspicious. She didn't want him showing up in town trying to find out what was wrong with her, and contacting him online seemed safer than calling him. He'd been able to get things out of her that she hadn't intended to disclose to anyone. She didn't feel safe talking to him right now.

"We are number twelve on the housing list Lila, so Darren says we should have a house in the next thirty days. He's excited, but I wish we could stay longer."

"I wish you could stay longer too, but we you know Darren is tired of all of this sister time. He wants some booty time with the good doctor." Lisa Laughed.

"You are so bad, but you're right. We need some privacy. Your room is too close."

"I know. I'm glad he gave us this time together. At least you're only going to be an hour away now. Who thought of putting a base 50 miles in the desert?"

"If you think about it Lila, it makes sense. They train with live ammunition sometimes. Do you think the town wanted them close enough to accidentally blow up a house or two?"

"I guess you're right. Did you get your license in the mail yet?"

"No I didn't. I better email the board. Thanks for looking out for me, missy."

Lisa dried her hands and went into her room to boot up her laptop. She had an appointment in two days with the hospital on post and needed her license for credentialing purposes.

"I want the copy you promised to put on my mantle, my sister the doctor," Lila said proudly. Darren came in just as Lisa got the state's home page up. She clicked on the link she needed and lifted her head for Darren's kiss.

"We need to go out and get you a car, doc. I could ride my bicycle to work, but I think it's time we get another car. I know you'll be traveling to visit Lila, and I don't want you broke down on the side of the road in my old Mercedes."

"Are you offering to buy me a car?" Lisa asked excitedly.

"If you hurry up. The offer is only good for three hours," Darren said holding up his checkbook.

"You don't have to ask me twice. Let me put on my sneakers and brush my hair, but why do I only have three hours?"

"The car dealership closes in three hours. Now move it, soldier."

"I'm getting a new car, Lila. You want to go hang out with an old married couple?" Lisa hollered to Lila who was on the couch munching potato chips in front of the television.

"No thanks. There is a good old movie on — Joan Crawford in **Queen Bee**. Joan Crawford is gangsta. I've never seen this one before." Lila went back to her movie. She didn't even notice when Lisa and Darren left the apartment. She was enjoying her Saturday on the couch in pee-jays with a tray of junk food. She knew it was bad for her, but she'd been really good up until now. She had chips, donuts and a plate of French fried potatoes. "A feast fit for a queen," Lila said, laughing at the timeliness of her comment. The phone rang just as Joan Crawford was telling Carol about her affair with her man. It was Samuel.

"Hello Samuel."

"Hey Lila, What's up with you? Have you gotten any of my messages?"

"Oh, I've been really busy. Sorry." Lila didn't want to talk or think of nice things to say. She had been on an emotional rollercoaster all week. All she wanted to do was go back to her movie and watch Joan destroy yet another life. She wanted to stuff her face with junk food and lose herself in someone else's life.

"You sound preoccupied with something else. I'll let you call me back. Later." Samuel hung up the phone. Lila clicked off the phone and threw it on the floor. She picked up the remote and hit play. "Good bye Samuel. Talk to you when I come back from La-La Land," she said, grabbing the bag of chips.

Samuel could not help but wonder if she had gone back to her lover.

CHAPTER 55

The phone was ringing when she opened her eyes again. This time it was Andrew. She grabbed the cell phone and clicked it on.

"Hey Andrew, it's been a while. What made you call me?"

"Lila, you are having my baby. I just wanted to see how you were getting along."

Lila stared at the cell phone before answering. "I'm fine, a little crazy but I think that's my hormones. I'm about to take leave soon so I can finally have this baby."

"Lila, did you know that Angie was pregnant too?"

"How could I miss it? She's all over the paper with you on her arm."

"I'm sorry about you and me, but Angie and I are really very happy now. I just wanted to see if there was anything I could help you with?"

"Or did you call to see if I'll be running through the streets of Juniper telling everyone that will listen how the mayor is having *two* babies in August?"

"Lila, I'm serious. I want to help if I can."

"I don't want to have this baby here. I want to go away somewhere. Can you help me with that?" Lila had thought about it long and hard. She didn't want to be in the same town when Angie had her baby. She wasn't in love with Andrew anymore, but it did hurt that Angie had him with her during her pregnancy and she had to keep her baby's paternity a secret. She was jealous of the attention that Angie was getting. After all, her baby was a part of the mayor's legacy too.

"Where do you want to go?"

"I don't know. You find somewhere. Call me and let me know when you find something. My sister is on her way back inside so I gotta go."

Andrew was confused and didn't know where he could send Lila to have her baby, but he had friends all over and would somewhere to send Lila. He was actually relieved she brought it up. He didn't want her to have the baby in town either.

Lila looked at Lisa and Darren when they came through the door. She wasn't very good at hiding her emotions. She pasted a smile on her face and asked if they were able to get a car. They had been successful, and Lisa was the proud owner of a Mercedes Benz Roadster.

The days seemed to melt into weeks, which melted into months, and before Lila knew it, she was in her eighth month of pregnancy. She put in for maternity leave four weeks earlier than the normal time because she now felt like a human basketball rolling back and forth to work. Andrew was giving her money monthly, and Lisa came down every weekend to do the house cleaning and grocery shopping. If it had not been for her sister's help and Andrew's financial support, she didn't know what she would do.

She talked with Samuel every week. He was working on a house and wasn't able to get to Juniper, but they had built a strong bond over the phone. Samuel had offered to pay for her to come to Kansas several times, but she had made one excuse after the other. There was no way out now. She had to tell Samuel soon what was going on. She picked up her cell phone and dialed his number. He answered on the first ring.

"Lila, I was just thinking about you. You just made my day." Lila hesitated before she began to speak. How could she tell Samuel that she had been hiding her pregnancy from him? "Are you still there, Lila?"

"Yes. I just wanted to hear your voice. I guess I'm feeling a little lonely today. I wish things were different and we were in the same place, together like regular couples." The tears began to fall. Samuel was an innocent bystander. She'd been the careless one, and now she had to suffer the consequences.

"Lila, you know I would come there if I could, but I..."

Lila interrupted before he could finish. Samuel heard more than Lila was saying, but he waited for her to speak again. Something was going on in Juniper. He wondered for the thousandth time in the last few months if she had gotten back with the man she was seeing before he came into her life.

"I'm not blaming you, Samuel. How's the house coming along?" She wanted to change the subject.

"It's going as planned, no major problems. I sent you something on Thursday. You should receive it today or Monday. Do you get packages from U.P.S on Saturdays?

"I don't know. I really never got anything from U.P.S." Lila couldn't remember ordering anything that had to be delivered to her apartment. She always had it sent to her job. It was easier and she didn't have to rush to the post office or the U.P.S. office to pick up her goods.

"What did you send?" Lila asked excitedly.

"I'm not telling. You'll see when it gets there. What you been up to?"

"Nothin' but work. My life is boring until you come here and make things happen."

Samuel laughed. "Why you trying to play me. You probably running wild without me to keep you in check."

"You'd be surprised." Angry at herself for not speaking up and telling him what she'd called to tell him, Lila told herself she'd do it when they next talked.

"Well you don't have long to play. The house will be done in two weeks, and then I'm coming to get you. How 'bout that?"

"That sounds like a plan. I feel better now. I'm going to get my clothes from the cleaners. I'll call you tomorrow," Lila lied. She had to end their conversation. If he was coming in two weeks, she didn't have much time.

"Okay love, 'til tomorrow. Later."

Lila clicked off the cell phone and paced the bedroom floor. "Oh God, what do I do now?" she shouted to the walls.

Andrew had agreed to send her away when she was ready. She was ready now. Neither her aunt nor her sister knew about her plans. She would tell them after she reached her destination, wherever that may be. Andrew hadn't told her yet.

He had been calling once a week t check on her. The next time he called she would tell him she was ready to leave town.

"Sorry Samuel, but I can't face you now."

CHAPTER 56

Angie rolled out of bed and slid into her slippers. Her back was killing her. She avoided the mirror as much as possible these days, even though everyone said she was a beautiful pregnant woman. All she saw in the mirror was a swollen face, a fat face. She was glad the misery was almost over. She had a plan to get back in shape as soon as she dropped her load. She and Andrew had decided not to ask the sex if the baby, but she prayed the baby was a boy so he could carry on the Blake name — no more babies were coming through her.

Her cell phone started chirping before she could slide on her housecoat. Andrew was already downstairs eating breakfast. She turned to pick up the phone and felt something warm and wet running down her leg. She ignored the phone and called out for Andrew. Something was wrong. She started for the bathroom, but the pain hit her hard. Andrew came through the door just as she fell to the floor.

"What happened? You're wet." Andrew picked up the phone and dialed Doctor Taylor. Her number was on a sticky on all the phones in the house. Angie was crying and Andrew was about to lose it. He was holding on to his hysterical wife and waiting for Doctor Taylor to answer the page. He sat on the floor and rocked Angie while they waited for a response. Doctor Taylor called within five minutes. Andrew snatched the receiver off the cradle.

"Hello, Doctor Taylor. Angie has had some kind of accident. I walked in and she was just landing on the floor."

The doctor wanted to talk to Angie, and Andrew handed her the phone.

"Doctor Taylor..."

"Tell me what happened, Angie?"

"I was going to answer my cell phone and felt something warm coming down my leg, and then I called Andrew. A pain hit me so hard I lost my balance and hit the floor."

"I want you to meet me at the hospital, okay? Put your husband on the phone." Angie handed Andrew the phone. She clung to him while he listened to Doctor Taylor, who told him to meet her on the OB ward. Andrew called Angie's mother and told her to meet them at the hospital.

The fifteen minutes it took to get to the hospital seemed like an hour to both of them. Mrs. Johnson was standing in front of the emergency exit when they arrived. Andrew rolled down the window and told her to get a wheelchair. He stopped the jeep and went to the other side and opened the door. Mrs. Johnson was back with a nurse pushing the wheelchair and Andrew helped Angie into the chair and watched as the nurse wheeled her away. Andrew jumped back into the jeep and pulled it into an empty parking space. In his haste, he realized he had forgotten his wallet and Angie's purse.

"Mister Mayor your wife is already on the OB ward," a young nurse said when he made it to the emergency room. He followed the signs to the OB clinic and tried not to think of what could be happening. He knew it was too early for the baby to come, but also knew that Angie was far enough along to have the baby without complications.

"Andrew," Mrs. Johnson said when he opened the door to the ward. She was standing near the nurse's station waiting for him.

"Doctor Taylor is already inside. They're in the birthing room down the hall.

"I've called my parents and they are on the way. Let's get in there and welcome our new addition to the family." Andrew hugged his mother-in-law and they entered the birthing room together. Angie was already in the birthing position, and Doctor Taylor was asking her to push. There was something going on that Andrew couldn't pick up on, and so he held Angie's hand and waited. The doctor removed their child and held it in one hand, hurriedly covering it and turning away from Angie and Alexander.

"We can't find a fetal heart beat," she said when she turned back around. He possibly passed away two weeks or so ago. Mister Blake, there is nothing we can do when the fetus dies before delivery. I'm sorry." Andrew tried to understand what Doctor Taylor was saying, but he was in shock. She must have told Angie prior to him entering the room because she didn't respond. She merely lay still with her tears rolling down her face. Now he knew what was going on. Their baby had died. He searched for words but none came to mind. It had been years since he felt tears on his face. "What happened?" he thought, too shocked to let the words leave his mind. Mrs. Johnson was consoling Angie, but no one could understand what she was going through, including Andrew.

"Mama, please talk to God — he knows you. Bring my son back, please. I'll do anything — please somebody help me. Don't take him from me. Oh God, Andrew. Make him wake up. Please. Please."

Andrew was helplessly staring at the little bundle in Angie's arms, which Doctor Taylor had just placed there. How could he help? He was just as broken as she was. He touched the top of the infant's head with his finger and felt the black curls that swirled around his head. "The boy is just sleeping. Someone made a mistake." Angie's screams woke him out of his daydream, alerting him to someone touching him.

"Mister Blake we're going to have to sedate your wife. She's going to make herself sick. I am so sorry for your loss. While she's resting, why don't you go into the other room and lie down? She won't know you're gone." Doctor Taylor reached for the needle the nurse had prepared and stuck Angie before showing Andrew to the sitting room.   "What happened? Did we miss something?" Andrew asked. Doctor Taylor knew these questions were coming, but as she had said in response every time she heard them, she replied that she just didn't know. They did the same series of tests every time this happened, and only in a few circumstances would a test positively identify what went wrong.

"I honestly don't know what happened. Angie didn't complain about the baby being still. She rescheduled her appointment for last week to this coming Friday, so it's been a week and a half since I checked her. The last time we visited, everything was fine. I know this sounds lame, but sometimes we never get an answer." Andrew shook his head and stretched out on the couch. Mrs. Johnson was sitting beside her daughter in the birthing room. The nurses had whisked the baby away for testing. Doctor Taylor went back to her office tired and broken hearted. She took the loss as a professional failure, always wondering if she may have missed something or forgotten to run a test or should have ordered another ultrasound. But she knew there was nothing to prevent sudden infant death. She had done everything she could to help produce a healthy happy baby.

CHAPTER 57

Lila could not seem to get comfortable in the hotel bed. She'd been in New Orleans a week and had tossed and turned every night. She'd made a terrible mistake in leaving Juniper, but it was too late to go back. She'd finally called her sister and aunt and told them where she was staying. Both were very upset with her for leaving without a word to them, but both assured her that they'd fly to New Orleans.

Lila couldn't shake the eerie feeling she got each time she entered the bedroom. She felt alone and scared. Someone was definitely walking over her grave, as she remembered her mother used to say. She visibly shivered and pulled her housecoat tighter. She sat at the desk in the small living room and pulled her cell phone out of her pocket. She clicked on the phone book and went down the list of names, searching for someone she could talk to. She'd talked to her aunt and her sister, but neither understood why she had left, but then, she couldn't explain it herself or they would know who fathered her child. Then she came across Crystal's name. She hesitated, then pushed the numbers. Crystal answered on the second ring.

"Lila, is that you? Are you okay? We've been worried sick about you. Where are you?"

"I'm in Louisiana."

"Louisiana? Why?"

"Crystal, I'm pregnant. I didn't have the heart to tell Samuel. He was so good to me. I don't want to give my baby up, and I can't ask him to raise another man's child."

"Lila, you didn't give him a chance to make a decision. You made it for him. You have to tell him what's going on."

"I can't, Crystal. Can you tell him for me and apologize. I never meant to hurt him, but I didn't want to see the disappointment in his eyes."

"Lila, that's something…" Lila cut her off.

"Crystal please, tell him. I know I won't get up the nerve, and I don't want him thinking that he did something wrong and that is the reason I haven't called."

Crystal let out a long sigh. She did not want to get into the middle of her brother's love life, but Lila sounded desperate. "I'll tell him Lila, but when he calls you, talk to him. I don't know what he'll say, but you're going to have to face him sooner or later."

"Thank you, Crystal. Kiss Jade for me." Lila was so relieved that Crystal would tell Samuel and the truth would finally be out.

"I will. Do you need anything, Lila?"

"No. I don't need anything. My sister and Aunt will be here tomorrow. I have a lot of explaining to do when they get here, so just remember me when you pray tonight."

"I'll do that. You take care of yourself, and remember to say your own prayer. Good bye."

Lila clicked the phone off and paced the hotel floor. Samuel was going to know everything soon, and she had to be prepared for his call — if he called. He could just choose to forget her. "Who wants a pregnant woman for a partner?" she thought as she lay down on the couch and drifted off into a deep sleep. Mysterious figures raced in and out of her dreams, causing her heart to beat rapidly. She couldn't make out their faces, but she felt as if she knew them. Glass crashed to the floor and doors slammed, causing her to toss and turn frantically to try and wake up.

"Lila, are you there?" Samuel knew she'd picked up because could hear the television in the background.

"Hi Samuel." She thought, "This is it," as she listened to the silence in the air.

"Why didn't you tell me about the baby?"

"I couldn't. It was too hard."

"You didn't trust me?"

"I am the one with the problem, not you."

"So you made a decision for me and went on without a word. I thought you wanted honesty, Lila?"

She remembered saying that but being honest about being pregnant with another man's child was different from being honest about feelings. She carried a new life within her that would be a part of their lives forever, if he chose to stay with her. "Doesn't he see the difference?" she thought as she tried to think of what to say.

"I can't do this..." Lila began to cry. She couldn't do a thing to change her situation, and talking about it with Samuel just made it worse.

"Lila. Talk to me."

"I messed up. The pill and everything... Just let it go. I wanted you to know that it wasn't something you'd done that made me go away. I considered an abortion, but I just couldn't; and I didn't want to choose between you and the baby, so I just decided to do this on my own."

"Crystal said you were in Louisiana. Is it because you don't want to face the father?"

"Something like that. I didn't want to be around anybody from Juniper.

"Do you want me to come down there?"

"Why? So you can tell me in person that it's over? Please, spare me."

"I know your family is joining you, but maybe if we could talk in person, you'd understand that I love you. I'm not pushing you into anything because I don't want you to make a hasty decision, but we need to talk. I just want the opportunity to address this in person. Can you understand that?"

"Yes."

"I'll see you tomorrow night. Goodnight Lila." Samuel clicked off the phone and slid it back into his pocket. He had some shuffling of his schedule to do if he wanted to be in Louisiana by tomorrow. He honestly didn't know what he'd do when he saw Lila pregnant. He just knew he had to go to her.

Lila pushed her plate away and said, "It's no use. I can't eat and pretend I'm not scared to death that Samuel will tell me it's over." Lisa and Barbara weren't very hungry either, and they pushed their plates aside and looked at Lila as if she'd lost her mind. Lisa spoke first.

"Lila, be careful. You sound as if you will fall apart if Samuel doesn't agree to keep seeing you. That's a dangerous place to be. Remember, our mother's problems started with her devotion to a man and the lack thereof for her children. Your focus has to be on yourself and on that baby you're carrying."

"You can get another man, but you cannot replace time lost chasing after someone who doesn't want to be caught. If Samuel says it's over, you will survive. I just don't think he's coming to Louisiana to say it's over," Barbara said, collecting the uneaten food and scraping it into the wastebasket.

"Drink your tea, Lila," Barbara said, but Lila was lost in her own world. She heard her aunt, but she'd got that eerie feeling again and tried to figure out what was happening.

"Auntie, I keep getting this funny feeling about this place, like something is going to happen to me."

Lisa and Barbara looked at each other. "Lila, I think you're just being paranoid. Go lay down. Samuel will be here tonight, and once you get past that, I think you'll be fine," Barbara said. Lisa shook her head in agreement with her aunt and went in to pull the covers back for Lila.

Lila followed Lisa into the bedroom and slid under the covers, but she couldn't shake the feeling that something was about to happen. She had not heard from Andrew in a week and wondered what was going on with him. She was tired of being pregnant and wanted the baby to come right away, but she was not due for another week. The isolation was getting to her. She pulled the covers up over her chin. It wasn't cold in the room, but she kept feeling a chill. At least her family had finally arrived. All she had to do was wait for Samuel to show up. "Then maybe the chills will go away," she thought as she hit the power button on the remote.

Lisa and Barbara discussed the fact that Lila had opted not to go into the hospital and was having a midwife deliver the baby. Neither liked the idea, but the plan had already been set in motion. Lisa called around to the hospitals to find out how to register the birth and to find out when they could bring the infant into the hospital to be tested for the usual things babies are tested for upon their arrival. Barbara set up the bassinette and put a few baby things inside the drawer. She hoped Lila would agree to go home with her and not back to Juniper. She was running from something in Juniper, and Barbara was afraid that something, or someone, would catch up with her.

There was no sound in the hotel room except for the six o'clock news and snoring from the corner where Barbara had curled up on the couch. Lisa and Lila sat on either side of the bed discussing the plan for the delivery in depth for the third time. Lisa was a medical professional and knew that midwives were competent and had become very popular again, but she still wished Lila would deliver in a hospital. This was Lila's first baby, and Lisa didn't want anything to go wrong. But Lila was determined to follow the plan that she and the mysterious father had set.

CHAPTER 58

Samuel arrived a little past midnight. Lila was ready to get the confrontation over with. All her fear was gone and she was prepared for the inevitable. She had worried long enough. If Samuel said he never wanted to see her again, she wouldn't blink an eye — she was too tired. But she didn't have to worry about a confrontation because she went into labor as soon as he stepped into the room. Lila dialed the number Andrew had given her and waited while the lady answered.

"Mrs. Cortez, please come now. This is Lila." Mrs. Cortez said she was on her way and hung up. Lila then dialed Andrew's number, but he did not answer. They had rehearsed what she would say if he was not available, and Lila spoke the words into the phone. She hoped Andrew would make it in time.

"Lila, this is obviously not the time to talk. I'll give you the privacy you need. I still love you, Lila. I couldn't say that until I saw you and knew in my heart that it was the truth. I still believe you're my promise, baby and all." Samuel kissed her forehead and said goodnight to Lisa and Barbara, who'd left the room so the couple could have their privacy. Lila was speechless. Either Samuel was insane or she was in a dream. Whatever the case, she was calm and ready to deliver. She was ready for whatever came her way now.

Mrs. Cortez showed up with a male escort, whom she introduced as Mister. She explained what was going to happen and started setting up. Barbara and Lisa followed her instructions while Mister sat on the couch in the other room and watched CNN as if he was in a trance.

CHAPTER 59

Andrew got Lila's message and hurried to pack. He had already called the airline to secure a seat. David was in New Orleans on business and would pick him up from the airport. It was David who supplied Andrew with the name of the midwife, and thus their plan had formed. David was going to be staying over for a visit with family members after he was finished with whatever business he was there to complete. David was always secretive about his trips, but Andrew did not question his actions. David had always been good to him. Angie was staying at her mother's house until she was well enough to function on her own. He had wanted to bring her back to their home, but he wasn't able to give her the care she needed. She was seeing a psychiatrist and heavily medicated.

Andrew had opted not to have a funeral for their son. There was a memorial with just the immediate family. The baby's body was not present, which Andrew thought was best, but a picture was placed on the mantle in their home and Mrs. Johnson's pastor came to deliver words of encouragement. Angie had sat through the ceremony like a stone statue. Her sisters cried and clung to her. They had never seen their sister in this state. After the ceremony, Angie followed her mother like a lost child. He had watched as she got in the car with her family without a look back at the house.

He was glad that she was with her family. It made it easier for him to go to New Orleans. Andrew wanted to be there for the birth. If the baby was born before he got there, he wouldn't mind, as long as the child was alive and healthy. He felt guilty about sneaking away to be with Lila, but he had to be there when his only child came into the world.

Mrs. Johnson looked all over the house for Angie. She had questioned the girls before they left for their jobs, but neither had seen Angie. They figured she'd wandered out to the backyard, as she did frequently, to sit and stare at nothing. Mrs. Johnson had forgotten about her daughter's backyard ventures when she still lived at home. She'd be out there at night sometimes looking at the stars. Angie had talked with her briefly about the pain she was feeling, but lately something else was bothering her. She had told her mother there was more to her pain than losing her son but would not go into detail.

Mrs. Johnson opened the screen door, but Angie was not sitting on the swing, her usual roost. Panic set in. There was probably a good reason why Angie was not in the backyard, but her mother needed to find her now. She went from room to room, but no Angie. She dialed Andrew's number, but his answering machine came on. She slipped on her shoes and grabbed her purse. Maybe she had gone home with Andrew and didn't remember to tell her. That was possible.

Angie's car was in the garage when Mrs. Johnson arrived, but Andrew's SUV was gone. She knocked, but there was no answer. Angie had to be with Andrew. Mrs. Johnson decided she would call him at work and on his cell phone until she reached him.

CHAPTER 60

Angie rushed through the terminal with the overnight bag she'd brought with her. All of the information she needed was in the note she found in Andrew's safe. During her brief stay at home before going to her mother's, he had assumed she was too drugged to notice that he was making phone calls and hiding papers everywhere. She had laid there, faking a drug induced sleep, when he opened his safe and slipped a paper inside. Before he could close it, Gayle called up and asked him to come quick. Someone was at the door asking questions, a reporter or someone from his office, she wasn't sure. When he left the room, she got up and opened the note, snapped a picture of it with her cell phone, and resumed the position she'd been in when he left. That was the day before the memorial for her little Andrew.

She did not look at the note until she reached her mother's home and was tucked into bed. Once everyone had gone to sleep, she read every line and discovered that, not only was her husband being unfaithful, but another woman was having his baby in New Orleans. The note was not from the woman, but from his friend David, information about a midwife and hotel and instructions on where he'd be waiting when he got to the airport. He had also left a code that the woman would use when she was in labor if Andrew couldn't be reached and either of them needed to leave a message. The midwife would call and say the same words to David.

Angie had slipped Andrew's phone off the nightstand while he went to say a few words to her mother before leaving for the airport. He was so sure she was mentally gone that he was being careless. The woman had left the code in his voice mail, and Angie knew it was time to move.

There were no direct flights available to New Orleans until the next night. So she booked a flight to Georgia, where she would have a four hour wait, then to New Orleans the following day. She wanted to do everything in her power to get there as early as she could. She'd waited until the five in the morning to sneak out and leave for the airport. She walked to the corner store where she called for a taxi. She'd call her mother when she got to Georgia.

Andrew had left David in the car to wait in the hotel parking lot. Andrew did not want to face Barbara, but he didn't have a choice. There was no way she'd stay away from her niece when she was giving birth. "I'm sorry" sounded so weak, but there was nothing else to say. The closer he had gotten to the room, the more he thought about the child he and Angie had lost, and the pain came rushing back like a bad dream.

Andrew stood up to pace the floor again. The cries were getting louder. The escort stared at the television screen, oblivious to the noise coming from the bedroom. Suddenly it was quiet, and the next thing he heard was the cry of a baby. He was so relieved that he fell back in the chair he was sitting in prior to pacing the floor. He'd forgotten that Barbara could come out at any moment and possibly attack him. Instead, the old woman came out with the baby wrapped in a pink blanket and placed her in Andrew's arms. Andrew kissed the small face and held the baby tightly. He knew her name, for Lila had told him several times after she discovered the sex of the child at her first ultrasound. Sarai lay quietly in his arms, sleeping soundly, unaware of the battle that was going on inside his heart. He was grieving for the loss of his son and overwhelmed with the little girl in his arms.

Andrew handed Sarai back to the old woman, pulled on his boots and coat, and rushed from the room and down the stairs to find David. The rain had stopped, but the streets were still full of water and the sky was still dark and angry. Once outside, he was able to understand what it felt like to be a father. He would protect Sarai with his life. Whatever he had to do to make her life full of love and laughter, he would do it. He was prepared to be a positive influence in her life, and if it meant he saw her on weekends and holidays, then he was prepared to make the sacrifice for her happiness.

CHAPTER 61

Lila rolled over and faced the window in front of her. She had given birth to a beautiful baby girl and wanted Samuel by her side. She dialed his extension and waited for him to pick up.

"Samuel, she's here, and she's so beautiful. I've been cleaned and rolled into a bun."

Misses Cortez had cleaned her and padded her before rolling her tightly inside the blankets on the bed. Sarai was bundled up as tight as Lila was and lying beside her. Lisa and Barbara were lying at the foot of the bed, asleep. They'd been up with her all night and took turns holding Sarai and cooing. Jet lag and plain old exhaustion had taken over, and both were sleeping as soundly as the baby.

"I'll be up in a minute." Samuel washed his face and brushed his teeth before leaving. He'd just finished showering and was putting on his pants before Lila called. Mrs. Cortez escorted him to the room where Lila was staring at Sarai as the baby slept. Samuel saw Lisa and Barbara snoozing at the foot of the bed and snickered.

"You'd think these two had the baby." He tiptoed around the bed to where Sarai lay. "She is beautiful, Lila."

"Thank you. Do you remember what you said before you left this morning?"

"I remember. Let me hold our baby." Samuel bent down and picked up the little pink bundle. Lila watched as he walked with her to the window and smiled down at her. He seemed sincere.

"Samuel."

Samuel turned from the window and waited for Lila to finish. "Will you marry me? I'm ready now. You are the man I've waited for all my life, and I just didn't know it."

"I'm going to tell our children how you forced me into marriage. If you're not ashamed, I'll marry you." He winked at Lila and placed the baby back in her place beside her mother. Then he sat on the edge of the bed, careful not to sit on Barbara's leg, and held Lila's hand.

"We can do this, Lila. I'm telling you that God is with us. Now I better get out of here so these ladies don't wake up and start screaming 'cause I'm lookin' at their morning faces."

"Okay. I love you, Samuel." She'd said it. She wasn't like Betty after all, incapable of loving someone. The moment the words left her mouth, she felt it in her heart. She almost begged Samuel to stay, but she knew he was right. Barbara and Lisa would die if they woke up and found Samuel in the room. She finally felt exhausted. She looked at Sarai to make sure she was sleeping. Lisa had made bottles and put them in a warmer for her. Lila lay back and went back to sleep.

Lisa was the first to get up and feed Sarai. Lila was knocked out. Barbara heard the baby and got up to see if someone was awake.

"Good practice for you, Miss Lisa," Barbara said, smiling.

"We don't want children until we own a home and have some of our bills paid off, but she's so cute and sweet, I almost want to have one as soon as possible."

"Lisa, did you see the man who came by to see Lila? I completely forgot to peek out and look at Sarai's father."

"I forgot to look too. I was so focused on what Mrs. Cortez was doing that I missed the opportunity. He didn't stay long. I wonder if he lives here."

"Well, he'd have to have just moved here. Otherwise, how would Lila know him? She hasn't been to New Orleans before."

"Can you believe Samuel still wants to marry her and raise Sarai?"

"Samuel is a good man. I've known him a long time. He's sincere."

"I'm glad. Now I hope she has sense enough to give him a chance." Lisa patted Sarai's back before putting her on the bed to change her pamper.

"She will. Hurry up so I can hold her before her mother wakes up and wants her. We gotta be careful not to spoil this little girl. She is so cute."

"Take her now. I'm going to call my husband before he starts to worry. He's a worry wart."

"I called Leonard when we got here. He's so busy that I don't even know if he heard what I said. He's covering for Samuel and trying to take care of himself too. You know I spoil him too."

"I'm sure Leonard will make it until you get back. Your house may be a mess, but he'll still be there."

Mrs. Cortez rapped lightly on the door frame before entering. "Me and Mistah gonna get somethin' ta eat. We'll be back shortly."

"Okay. She'll be fine. Take your time," Barbara answered as she rocked Sarai in her arms. She hadn't thought about food until that moment, but they could order something from room service later. She wanted to wait until Lila woke up again so she could order for her too.

CHAPTER 62

Lila and the baby did well through the night, but when morning came, Lisa and Mrs. Cortez agreed that Sarai looked yellow. Lisa called the hospital and was told to bring the baby in through the emergency room. Lisa assured Lila that jaundice was a common ailment in new infants, and she told her that a couple of days under an ultraviolet light or in the window with direct sunlight would cure it. She had to take the baby in to get her levels checked first, however, so the doctors would know what was needed.

Lila told her aunt to go along. She had been cooped up in the hotel the whole time she'd been in New Orleans. Going to the hospital was not a fun trip, but at least she would see something other than the same four walls. Barbara agreed. Lila was doing fine and able to get to the bathroom and back to the bed by herself, and Samuel was right down the hall if she needed anything. Lila was going to spend her time sleeping. Soon, everyone would have to go home and she would be left to care for Sarai. She decided to take advantage of the help she was getting.

Lila took her shower before the others left for the hospital. She could manage going to the bathroom while they were gone, but she didn't want to chance falling in the shower while they were away. She then slid under the covers for her nap. She heard a light rap on the door before she fell asleep. "Maybe Lisa or Aunt Barbara forgot to take the key," she thought as she made her way to the door. Andrew was standing in the hall when she opened the door. She moved to the side and let him in.

"How are you doing?"

"I'm doing better today. I'm still sore but doing good," Lila said, easing herself down in the chair by the door.

"Where is Sarai?" Andrew asked, looking around.

"My sister took her to the hospital. She looked a little yellow and needed a quick checkup."

"She's not here?" Andrew seemed agitated.

"Did you just hear me? She needed to be checked."

"I'm sorry. I have a lot on my mind. My wife is missing, and I have to get back to Juniper. Our son died before he was born, and it really broke Angie up. I didn't want to mention that until after you had Sarai."

"Oh God, Andrew. I'm sorry. My family is here to help with the baby. You go back and try and help her. I know how I'd feel if something happened to Sarai…" Lila was stopped in mid-sentence by another knock at the door. She nodded for Andrew to open the door. He pulled the door open.

"This is your secret, Andrew. You brought this little girl cross country to have your baby. Did you think I was too stupid to put two and two together?" Andrew was so shocked he couldn't move. Lila tried to get up and move back into the bedroom, but Angie blocked her path. She didn't recognized Angie at first. Her hair was pulled back in a ponytail and she wore a baseball hat and had on a jogging suit. She didn't have on any makeup and looked as if she was on heavy drugs.

Andrew finally came to his senses and tried to reach out to touch Angie. She pulled away and started for the bedroom.

"Where is the baby? The proud parents should be ready to show her off."

Lila looked helplessly at Andrew. She was in no condition to tangle with a half-crazed wife. Then Andrew followed Angie, begging her to leave with him and he would explain everything. He managed to drag her away from the bassinette and motioned for Lila to get into the room while he tried dragging Angie away. Angie rambled on and on about the missing baby and fought with Andrew to get loose. Andrew was still trying to get her out of the room when Angie turned to him and smiled.

"I want that baby, Andrew. She's mine. That girl can't have your baby. I'm your wife, not her."

Lila opened her mouth to speak, but the first of three bullets hit before a sound could escape her lips. She was falling to the floor. No one could hear the muffled shots, but she felt them. Bodies moved in slow motion out of the room. Marcus entered the room and told them to hurry to the car. "Why would Marcus be with Andrew?" she thought as the bodies made their way out of the hotel room. She dragged herself to the phone and dialed Samuel's room number.

"Help me, Sam…"

CHAPTER 63

The hospital room was quiet except for the beeping of the machines that were sustaining Lila's life. One bullet had nicked her kidney, another just missed her heart, and the third was just a flesh wound to her thigh. The doctor said she was lucky to be alive, but Samuel knew she had been covered by his prayers. He'd rushed to the room and found her in the fetal position on the floor. The police questioned him at length, but all he could tell them was that, when he arrived, Lila was in the room alone and a midwife and her escort were in the room the night before. Lila was able to tell them who was in the room with her right before she was shot, but she didn't know who pulled the trigger.

Lisa and Barbara were still in the hospital when Lila was brought to the emergency room. The pediatrician advised them to leave Sarai on the ward for observation. Lisa was calling Lila to explain why Sarai was admitted, but Samuel answered and delivered the bad news. They rushed to the emergency room, but Lila was already in surgery.

Lisa was a basket case, and Barbara was consoling her as she tried to be brave herself. The anger she felt when she found out that Andrew was the father had ripped through her like a knife. He was a friend as well as her employer when she worked at City Hall. She felt betrayed. She had spoken to him on several occasions since she left, and he hadn't once mentioned Lila's name. She had unknowingly led her niece into this den of iniquity. The police had put a warrant out for the arrest of Andrew and Angela Blake, but Lila had told them Marcus was there. Barbara had explained to them that Lila might have been slipping in and out of consciousness and saw Marcus in one of her nightmares.

David climbed behind the wheel and fired up the big rig. He knew his aunt would keep her mouth shut about Andrew staying with them. Andrew and Angie hid behind the boxes he'd put in the truck bed. No one was looking for him, so he'd be able to get them somewhere safe.

"Angie, we have to go back and face the police. We can't run forever."

Angie was sitting in the corner of the truck rocking. She didn't know what to do. Everything had gone so wrong. She was just going to scare the woman with the gun and take the baby. Nobody was supposed to get hurt. Andrew was telling her they needed to turn themselves in, but she just wanted to go back home and start all over again. Andrew got as close as Angie would allow him and tried to reason with her.

"I messed up, Angie. I couldn't tell you that she was pregnant. I didn't want to hurt you like that." Angie scooted farther away when Andrew tried to touch her. Let me get you some help. We have to turn ourselves in." Angie watched as Andrew dialed David's cell number and asked him to find the nearest police station.

This is how it was going to end — both of them locked in a jail cell. Angie was past crying. She welcomed the idea of a jail cell. There were no decisions to make and she didn't have to lie when people came around asking how she felt. She made one request of Andrew before withdrawing back to her corner.

They were fifteen minutes from Baton Rouge. David dialed information and found out how to get to the nearest police station. Andrew got out and carried Angie inside. He explained who he was and why they had come in. An officer called New Orleans and let them know that they had their suspects and was told a detective would be there shortly to escort them back to New Orleans. Andrew's heart sank when the female officer came to escort Angie to a holding cell.

"Don't let me down, Andrew," Angie said before she was escorted to the back He shook his head and got up to hug her, but Angie backed away. She had decided there would be no more physical contact. She reasoned, "Why make things worse than they were? She refused to call her mother back for the same reason. Only the living needed hugs and words of encouragement. She was as dead as her son. Everything had been stripped away from her. She couldn't even grieve with her husband. He had another woman and child. The cell would be a welcome barrier against love, hope and encouragement. No one could get to her without her consent, and she would never give it.

CHAPTER 64

The ***Desert Den's*** headline on September thirtieth, two thousand and one stopped traffic. Mayor Andrew Blake was found dead in his home. A suicide note was found next to the body. Andrew's father had come to check on his son because he hadn't heard from him and he wasn't answering his cell or house phone.

Mayor Blake had been dead for at least two days according to the coroner. The article stated that the mayor was distraught over the loss of his son and his wife being committed to a mental hospital after she was charged with attempted murder. The people of Juniper were in shock when the paper came out. They knew the mayor was upset, but no one knew he was suffering so badly.

The doors of City Hall were closed for the funeral of the man who was colleague and friend to those who worked there. People shook their heads and consoled each other on the way out of the church. Andrew and Angie's families exited the church through the back door to avoid the reporters waiting outside the service. Juniper was a nondescript town just two hours from Las Vegas, but with the news of attempted murder, suicide by a city official, and rumors of affairs, the town was crawling with reporters looking to capitalize on a story. A scout from a popular television series that spotlighted women who kill was in town asking to buy the rights for an upcoming episode.

Jaynell and Tanya followed the families out of the back door. Neither wanted a camera shoved in their faces. Angie was their friend, and they would honor their friend with their silence.

Lila stared at the computer screen where the images of Andrew on the front page of the ***Desert Den's*** web site looked back at her. Joe had sent her an email explaining what happened and attached the link to the story. Lila scrolled down and read the horrible account of Andrew's final day. She could only imagine the pain he was going through when he pulled the trigger. She wiped a tear away and closed the email message. She went down to the kitchen to look for her Aunt to give her the bad news.

There was a note from her aunt letting her know she'd gone to the grocery store, and beside the note was Lila's mail. She idly sifted through the small stack and stopped when she saw the name and return address on the last letter in the stack, Andrew Blake. The letter seemed to way a ton. She hurried back to her room and sat down at the computer. He must

have written the letter right before that day. Lila slowly opened the
envelope and read the contents.

Dear Lila,

I know you've heard the news by now, but I had to
write you and explain myself. There are going to be
a lot of stories going around, but you should know
the truth. I made a promise to Angie the day we
turned ourselves in to the police, but I couldn't go
on allowing her to be blamed for something I'd done.
I pulled the trigger that day in the hotel. Angie
only came to scare you and take Sarai, but when the
baby was not in the room and I dragged her away,
Angie went limp in my arms.

I wanted to give her something to hold on to so
I wouldn't lose her, and in that moment, I thought
if you were gone we could raise Sarai and be a
family. I lost my head for a minute. If you could
have seen how desperate and lost Angie was, you'd
understand what I was trying to do. I'm not asking
for your forgiveness for myself but for Angie.
She's innocent. Angie told me that, if I didn't let
her suffer in jail, she would kill herself as soon
as she got back to Juniper. I didn't know what to
do, so I agreed. But I can't live with the lie
anymore. I've tried to see her, and her mother and
sisters have all tried as well, and she has refused
us all.

I sent a letter to the detective who handled our
case and told him the whole story. I didn't want
you dead. I wanted Angie to live. Last of all,
enclosed are accounts for Sarai's care and a special
account for her when she reaches the age of twenty-
one.

I don't know what you'll tell her when she's old
enough, but we did have some good times. You let
her know I fell in love with her the first time I
saw her and she was not a mistake. I wanted her.
Do me one last favor: make sure you take her to see
my parents. Send them pictures and allow them to be
part of her life. They shouldn't miss out on their
only grandchild because of my mistakes.

Finally Lila, take care of yourself and our
daughter. I wish you the very best that life has to
offer.

Sincerely,

PostPartum

Andrew Blake

Lila put the other contents of the envelope on the computer desk and walked over to the crib where Sarai lay asleep. She looked very much like her father and even had the same birthmark on her shoulder that he had. Andrew was not the only one to blame for their problems. She was just as much to blame as he was. She knew he was married and she continued to go after him. He'd even tried to avoid her early on, but she kept coming back. It was too late to tell him she was sorry. So many lives were torn apart because of the actions of two selfish people, herself and Andrew.

But Sarai would not suffer because of their mistakes. Andrew was a good man and she would tell her that. And yes, she would send pictures to his parents and even invite them for a visit. Going back to Juniper wasn't something she had planned to do for a long time, but she would, to answer Andrew's request.

In spite of everything that had happened, Lila still had hope for her future. She and Samuel were seeing their pastor for counseling, and just before Christmas — they hadn't set an exact date yet — they were getting married.

Lila followed her Aunt's advice and went to church with Samuel whenever she felt like it. He didn't push her, and suddenly, without asking, she was a regular. She'd even started a breakfast program for the Sunday school children. Every Sunday right before children's church, Lila and her small staff would cook a hot meal for the children. Aunt Barbara was one of her staff members. Leonard had even showed up a couple of Sundays.

Lila couldn't help thinking about Angie. She wanted to reach out to her, but she knew that might not be a good idea considering their present circumstances. She prayed that one day Angie would be well enough to leave the hospital and start her life over again. She was a living witness that, with God all things are possible.

The Bonds Of Iniquity

It had been five years since she'd been outside the gates of Woodlawn on her own, but she had been a model patient and now the psychiatrist had declared her sane. It took her a year, but she finally broke her silence. She had followed every instruction and repeated only the things that they wanted to hear. She had even endured the abuse inflicted by one of the aides on her floor, but he'd proved to be very useful to her in gaining items needed for her new life. She knew her secret was safe with him. He had too much to lose by talking. It was amazing how many criminals worked for the correctional system.

Everything had changed drastically since she'd retreated from the civilized world. New houses and businesses had sprung up all around the city. The Indian Casino had brought prosperity to the city, but with it came people looking for a million dollar dream who had instead lost their life savings and were camped out on the streets waving signs for food, work, and other necessities. She'd read the paper faithfully each day, and it was full of the hard luck stories the casinos had created.

None of that mattered to her. She had no intention of staying in Juniper. Her life had been snatched away from her five years ago, and it was time to get it back. The city had placed their household items in storage after her husband's tragic death. Everyone was kind and spoke words of encouragement to her. She nodded appropriately and demurely bowed her head and whispered, "Thank You." There was no reason for them to pity her. A new life was on the horizon for her. She turned to Jaynell and smiled.

"No one but you knows my life plans, and you won't tell, will you Jay?" She didn't wait for her friend to answer before she started talking again. "Andrew, I'm going to get our baby back. I know you'd want me to have her. Jaynell is going to help me, so don't you worry. I'll find that girl and I'll get our baby back."

Angie finished packing the last suitcase and looked back at Jaynell. She couldn't leave her behind. She drug out the large black trunk that she'd kept her pillow in during her days as His Honor's wife. Those days were gone. The linens had been packed in boxes and stored with their other things. She had no need for those things now. She only selected a few items and asked that the rest be given to charity.

"Now Jay, I want you to be a good girl and be still while I wrap you up. I don't want anyone to know you're in here. Things won't go well for me if they find you. Angie poured the dry ice inside the bottom of the trunk. She got the boxes of plastic wrap and began at Jaynell's feet and worked her way up to her head. She gently pulled her eyelids down but couldn't wrap her head. She lay a couple of sheets over the dry ice for Jaynell's head. She rolled the computer chair that Jaynell lay slumped in over to the trunk and poured the body inside.

Jaynell had told her she needed to go back to Woodlawn after she explained her plans to her. She kept saying that the baby belonged to the other woman. Angie grew weary of her constant nagging about getting more help. "Did Jaynell live at Woodlawn thousands of miles away from home? Did her husband commit suicide? Did her mother die while she was away? Was she assaulted and raped by an aide that was supposed to be a caretaker? No, all of those things happened to Angela Blake, not Jaynell Henderson," she muttered to herself.

Jaynell had said she was going to call the hospital if she didn't get help. Angie couldn't allow her to do that, and so she came up behind her and slammed the skillet down hard to the back of her head. Jaynell slumped to the floor and never got up again.

She'd rented a truck that had an automatic drop for large items and a complimentary hand truck. Once she was far enough out of town, she would dispose of Jaynell's body.

She only needed to make one stop: in Black Rock to visit the grave of her husband. She'd already visited the graves of her father and son. Andrew needed to know she was going to get their daughter. He'd be proud of her. He always wanted a family.

GJ Coleman is originally from Brooklyn, New York and is presently living in Southern California with her husband and three of their five children. PostPartum is her first Novel.

PostPartum

www.ingramcontent.com/pod-product-compliance
Lightning Source LLC
Chambersburg PA
CBHW051828170626
46807CB00003B/1073